D0850882

Beyond Infinite Healing

Also by DH Parsons

The 60s
Life ain't Nothin' but a Slow Jazz Dance
1967 San Francisco:
My Romance with the Summer of Love
The Muse: Coming of Age in 1968

Lifestyle and Inspirational
Eat Yoga!
Book of Din

All available on Amazon

The Diary

of **Mary
Bliss
Parsons**

Volume 3

Beyond Infinite Healing
A Promise from Above

Second Edition

D H Parsons
Elise R. Brion

Beyond Infinite Healing

Second Edition

This edition contains considerably more material and deeper insights than the previous version.

Copyright 2020 by DH Parsons

**Editing, layout, and design by Susan Bingaman,
Bliss-Parsons Publishing, Columbia, MO**

Bliss-Parsons Institute, founded by DH Parsons, is devoted to the exploration and expression of Truth, with the intent to guide as many people as possible toward Right Living and the healing of spirit, soul, and body.

All rights reserved

No part of this book may be reproduced or transmitted in any form or by any means without the written permission of the author and publisher.

ISBN: 978-1-948553-09-4
Library of Congress Control Number: 2020902293

CONTENTS

PREFACE: THE PORTAL IS OPENED

There is a moment in space when all time stops because the Presence of God is sensed so strongly that all limitations, constructs, and human belief systems are simply abolished for a brief instant within the third dimension known to Earth's residents. There is a moment when the fullness of Healing within the God's Truth and Unconditional Love is so permeating, and so deeply and purely felt, that there is no turning back to the ways of one's former identity, or the world's dictation of how life and reality are supposed to behave. There is the moment when the tiniest of miracles suddenly acknowledged, becomes the magnitude of impossibilities made manifest in this three-dimensional plane. This moment has been infused into each and every word of *Volume Three* of *The Diary of Mary Bliss Parsons*.

We offer you our extended hand and welcome you to step into the embrace of that which goes *Beyond Infinite Healing*, for this is our *Promise from Above*.

INTRODUCTION

Annie has directed me to write about this subject early in *Volume Three* of *Mary's Diary*. Annie is, of course, much more than my daughter; she is a repository of information that goes way beyond the scope of the human mind. I learned a long time ago never to ask why of anything she asks of me.

Elise, the Strong Weet you met in *Volume 2: The Lost Revelation*, joins with me again, in the writing and transmission of this knowledge from Mary, Annie, and the Mother of Humanity, known to you more commonly, yet inadequately, as Mother Nature. This volume of the Diary differs a bit from the first two. Whereas *The Strong Witch Society* and *The Lost Revelation* were concerned primarily with the introduction of specific individuals and the conveyance of Mary's primary message — that this world is in a serious state that must be rectified quickly or all will be lost — this volume contains information that can be used by all to not only change themselves and the culture for the better, but to enable the Creation Frequency to heal, thus saving the planet.

Also contained in this volume are entries devoted to what Annie calls corrective knowledge. The readers will be able to apply this instruction to heal their own life-frequency and to enhance the precision of their resonance with the Creation Frequency. The results will contribute greatly to the healing of this world and speed the personal healing of others applying the powerful principles offered here.

Volume Three of *The Diary* is a hands-on, how-to

instruction manual for the Weet and for anyone else on this world choosing to heed its teachings and apply them to their own lives. It contains common sense instructions, as well as knowledge never before gifted to this world. Both are necessary. Do not make hasty judgments regarding the nature of anything presented herein. Read carefully and consider the meanings behind the words; they will instill within your soul new life and understanding of all that you are now and that you can become. There are lessons to learn and miracles to witness in nearly every entry found upon these pages.

The heart of the matter

In order to prepare oneself to receive the limitlessness of God's healing, and while it is still possible, to create Heaven here on Earth, it must be understood that humanity, in and of itself, is not divine. The divine realm of God cannot be claimed by any earthly being. It is a serious and destructive personal block for any single individual to think that he or she is naturally and inherently comparable to the absolute perfection of God. It is, however, within the birthright of each and every person to be able to awaken to certain qualities and characteristics that are gifts from the heart of God and given to all humankind. These gifts are love, joy, peace, patience, kindness, goodness, faithfulness, gentleness, and self-control. No person on this Earth, regardless of ethnicity or nationality, is born into a world where these energies are modeled. It is the challenge of each human's lifetime to see through the negativity and evils that have been imprinted into the collective mindset and to reclaim, reconnect, and receive that which comes exclusively from God. Negativity has permeated the physical realms of man and must be overcome. Disconnected thinking has become the fuel that drives the human constructs of the conscious mind, education, religions, government, subcultures, and races. Mankind has chosen to disconnect human thought from the Will of God.

These are difficult realities to face, but this cultural mindset, insidiously severed from the Will of the Creator God, must be overcome. This is the only way to bring oneself back into proper harmonic vibration with the Creation Frequency, so that the mind and body can heal.

Volume Three of *The Diary of Mary Bliss Parsons* embodies our cosmic effort to bring humanity back to living in pure truth, and unconditional love. This book contains much important and life-changing information that has never before been revealed to this world. Read the words carefully. Believe them and take them inside you. That is the key to all healing and personal growth. Jesus clearly taught that healing comes from belief. Believe what He taught.

THE IMPORTANCE OF RIGHT THINKING

To the average person, a positive state of well-being means that one is content with the surroundings of one's life, is in possession of reasonably good health, and that one is happy in most circumstances. In reality, it means much more. In the purest sense of the word, to be *well* means to be *whole*. So, a more correct definition for well-being would be a condition of *wholeness* down to the core of one's very being, commonly referred to as *self*.

Wholeness implies more than physical health, wealth, or even happiness as a state of being. Well-being, or wholeness, concerns itself with completeness of being—of everything that makes you You—all of which constitutes self. Self is not the outside image of your physical persona, it is the true reality of who you really are on the inside.

It must also be mentioned that no human being, in and of him or herself, is God. The self that we are speaking of is the self that was gifted to an individual by God when that individual was created. The created self, indeed, does have some of the operational qualities that are similar to a minute portion of the qualities possessed by God, but those qualities in no way make the *created* equal to the *God*. This is an important point, for there are some within the human culture who believe that a Creator God does not exist, and that humans are capable, in and of themselves, of achieving personal perfection as well as a so-called enlightened cultural consciousness, for the purpose of creating their own perfect world. This exclusion of the existence of the independent Creator God from the belief system of this world is one of the two primary reasons for the countdown to destruction this world now faces.

Self is part of the complete picture and, at the same

time, self is whole. Nothing is missing in self. Nothing is sick in self. Nothing is not working in self. Nothing has been left out of self. The pieces are all there. Everything is perfect and eternal. Self, sometimes referred to as soul or being, is whole and complete.

The conscious being, which can also be referred to as personality, is controlled by two things: conscious mind and ego, both of which interchange with each other, and each maintains the other's existence. The problems found within the societies of Earth today are not caused by gods or demons, nor are they caused by anything spiritual or supernatural, as many religions profess. They are caused by the imbalanced energy frequencies being released from the incomplete minds and confused egos, of the totality of mankind. The self does not stir up anything on this planet. The self is, indeed, in direct contact with God, Who is, as agreed upon by nearly every credible faith on Earth, foremost among other things a Spirit of love, peace and understanding. In the Christian New Testament, the Apostle John states clearly in 1 John 4:8, that *God is love*. By revealing this, John did not intend for humanity to believe that love is all that God is. Love is merely one of the innumerable attributes of God, many of which humankind lacks the ability to even discover, let alone understand, dissect, and form opinions and religions about. Yes, God is as close as your own heartbeat, and you can develop a personal contact with God through your own thoughts and prayers, but it goes beyond mere arrogance for any human being to compare him or herself with God, Who is infinitely beyond simple human nature. It borders on self-worship, which, as Mary has revealed clearly in her *Diary*, is not a good idea.

Because of the ingrained attribute of love, it is impossible for either an individual self, or the communal selves of an entire culture, to destroy the well-being of a person, nation, religion, or even planet. If our self is made in the image of God, logic dictates that our self will reflect God's gifts of peace, love, and understanding. If something about us is out of kilter, it has nothing to do with self; it is our conscious mind that is defective in some way. If a nation, culture, or religion is out of kilter, or at war with each other, that can only mean that the accumulated minds/egos of that nation, culture, or religion are not whole or healthy. They are out of balance. In order for a human mind to be whole and healthy it must be taught a Higher Truth.

Mary and Annie have each stated several times in the previous volumes of *Mary's Diary* that the Higher Truth that governs everything in this universe must be taught, correcting the errors learned from and reinforced by the common culture. They also affirmed that this Higher Truth must be applied as well if all things are to be in balance and harmony and so run smoothly. If not, things will run badly, or they will not run at all. This is the secret to solving nearly every problem facing mankind today.

To say that individuals hurt each other for ethical reasons is to defy logic, as the presence of ethics would imply the absence of harm. To say that wars are fought for religious reasons is ludicrous. Wars are not fought for any reasons of a higher nature, wars are fought because of wrong thinking—and wrong thinking is a product of human mind/ego.

Both sides in all altercations may sincerely think they are in the right, and therein lies the problem—they only *think* they are right, and the conscious thinking process of the human mind has a problem. The human capacity to think is limitless. A person can literally sit around day in and day out just thinking, and his/her brain and mind will indiscriminately store away for future use every single thought. Every single bit of information — good, bad, or indifferent — is retained in the physical memory bank.

What's the problem with that? The problem is, that unless a person applies the filters of the Higher Truths and Laws to this physical store of information and ideas, that person will not know how to most effectively use all of the information he or she has stored. The result may be — and often is — that the information is used in non-productive and even harmful ways.

Consider what happens when raw information is used without the control of Higher Truth. The predictable result is the lack of stability of nearly everything within a society. The far-reaching and often devastating result can be a serious imbalance of human emotions and reactions, which may lead to war, corrupt government, and out of control morality — the state in which mankind finds itself today.

None of this is the fault of self, or of God Who creates and sustains the self of every human being on this planet and on all planets throughout all the universes in existence. Certainly, none of these drastic results can be justified by the claim that it was done in God's name. They lie at the feet of wrong thinking within the minds of human beings.

The only way an individual can change wrong thinking into right thinking is to make the conscious decision to monitor the information put forth by the confused culture in which they live and entering into their mind. If a human is to gain perfect health, the only information that can be allowed into the mind is that which comes from the Higher Truth of God. The chaotic, arbitrary, polluted, depraved, and dangerous thoughts of a society governed by flawed thinking and dishonest activity are the very things that are distorting the Creation Frequency and will lead to dire consequences if the situation is not corrected soon.

The decision of a single individual to change from wrong to right thinking will go a long way toward the correction of their own personal energy frequency, allowing it to realign with the Creation Frequency. If a majority of individuals residing on this world make that same decision, the cumulative results, added to the efforts of the Strong Weet, can bring about the correction of the Creation Frequency that baths this world with life, and Mary's dire predictions will not be realized.

It is indeed possible for each individual to personally achieve this goal.

The Apostle Paul gave us the first step toward achieving that end. In Romans 12:2, he instructs us to "... be transformed by the renewing of your mind ..." The word *transform* means to change. *Renew* means to get rid of the old. Wrong thinking is the result of being unwilling to do either of these. This is where ego comes into play, because it is ego that derails the efforts of a person to renew his/her mind. This verse is another way of telling people to get rid of old opinions, past prejudices, shallow attitudes, and false teachings that have resulted in the state of mind in which they find themselves today. Just dump them and start all over. People must be willing to do this, or it will be impossible for them to truly transform, and they will remain in this life as flawed individuals. As a result, there will always be wars and corruption and serious problems.

Hence the reason to heed the morals, ethics and higher truths that come from God by way of the Creation Frequency, rather than relying on the guesses and musings of mankind. Hence the reason for Mary's Diary, and for the Weet, who will help to teach the Higher Truths in ways that everyone can understand, undistorted by politics and greed. There are two simple steps that individuals and humanity as a whole can take that will lead to the well-being of all:

Repair the damage done to human society by erroneous teaching and

Agree to learn and promote new Truths that will change the world for the better.

The two main problems haunting the history of every culture on Earth are first, all your cultures are teaching the wrong things, and second, the individuals within the cultures have been conditioned over the centuries to be suspicious of any teaching that is not found within the confines of the accepted and they have become hostile to learning the Higher Truth. It's easier to stay the same and not make waves. It's easier to be like everyone else, because when individuals march to a different beat, it often means they will be marching alone and unprotected from whatever comes at them from a hostile environment.

Yes, at first glance, your world does appear to be a mess. Terrorism is rampant; your religions are at war with each other; every nation on earth seems to be quarreling with at least one other nation; your politicians have become dishonest, embarrassingly predictable, and their leadership no longer commands the respect it once did; your whole structure of life seems to have crumbled in the mediocrity of your own confused state; political correctness has replaced common sense. All of this does seem to paint a rather bleak picture. The reality is that *everyone* on Earth is a part of the problem. The good news is this: God has promised humanity that it will not take the majority of the world's population acting together to solve the problem.

Neither God nor Mother H have revealed how much of the population of the planet must change their wrong thinking into right thinking in order to save it, but they have assured humanity that the number set is attainable, and when that goal is reached, the life and health of planet Earth will quickly and dramatically change and for the better. Together we can reset the world.

Once again, if humanity is to change for the better, then humans must first be willing to change, but sadly, there are many who are unwilling to do so. This reluctance can be traced back to three primary causes:

1. PERSONAL POWER: Power does corrupt, and this corruption can attack any level of your culture from politics to religion.
2. EGO: It is said that pride comes before a fall, and this is generally the case. However, so many within your culture refuse to pay attention to the wisdom found within this saying. A few lessons in humility learned and practiced in daily life by everyone would be of great benefit.
3. LAZINESS: Exceeding the fault of physical laziness, is intellectual laziness. One can never perfect the art of right thinking when one is incapable of controlling one's thoughts due to mental laziness.

None of the above problems are reasons for those who are of higher awareness to give up on bringing positive change into a negative scenario. The more good that is accomplished by a person, the more positive energy is released by that person into his or her own sphere of existence. The result is that their goodness will take root and grow in those around them.

This effect has been widely noted and is known by several different names such as the ripple effect and—Annie's personal favorite—the butterfly effect. The most important aspect of this phenomenon is that it all begins with you. You can be the pebble in the pond or the butterfly that starts a global change. You can create the ultimate blessing that can unleash the powers of the Creation Frequency. You can bring forth from the very depths of your inner self a spiritual frequency that will permeate the illusory mist of negativity that has enshrouded mankind's true purpose through the centuries so that many have forgotten their true nature.

Is it possible that you will be the catalyst for the Great Change that must come soon to this planet? It is more than just possible, it is as promised by God:

You did not choose me, I chose YOU and appointed YOU that YOU should go and bear fruit ... (John 15:16)

Do not merely read the words of this book. Study them. Open your hearts and your minds to the message from above that lies within every page of *Beyond Infinite Healing*. Become everything you were originally designed to become and enter into a new life that promises more than a human mind can ever grasp.

"Before I formed you in the womb I knew you, and before you were born I consecrated you ..." (Jeremiah 1:5)

ANNIE IN THE MIDDLE OF THE NIGHT

It is 2 AM, and neither my Father, nor Elise has any idea I am writing this right now. But they won't mind. They have done a wonderful job of opening up something that is of great importance to you all, and I want you to be aware of this. I want you to read VOLUME THREE with your real vision — the vision that comes from the heart. Your heart-vision is infinitely more sensitive than your ocular vision and will convince you that what Father and Elise are sharing with you on the pages of this book comes directly from God. You will be reminded of truths that your soul already knows, but you must allow Father, Elise, and me, to assist you in clearing away the cobwebs that have gathered over the years. There is so much to be discovered beyond the windowpane of your own mind, and even beyond this cosmos. Join with us as we lead you through the pages that follow to discover what lies BEYOND INFINITE HEALING.

I hear Father turning in his sleep, so I must be on my way. I am going next door to visit Elise and to whisper a few things into her ear while she sleeps.

ELISE OPENS THE BOOK OF LIGHT

Upon waking after a night of Annie dancing around in my head, I needed to collect myself and focus so that I could begin to write, but something unusual caught my eye immediately after I sat up in bed. Sitting on my computer keyboard is an old, dusty, leather-bound book. Most certainly not one that I placed there, as I don't own such a book. The mysterious thing looks like it could have come from the Alexandrian Library. Things often appear from out of nowhere here. This had to be Annie's doing. I feel compelled to pick it up and read. The one thing I am sure of is that this book will in some way further assist in clarifying the details of The Great Plan.

The moment my eyes fall upon the first page, it happens. At first, it is a feeling. The words shoot through me with a sensation like nothing I have ever experienced. Like my own deep inhalation, the words enter my head and permeate every part of my brain. It is as if my brain is moving outside the confines of my skull. I read on. Something inside me is yearning for more, drinking in this nourishment as someone starved and dehydrated in a foreign world finding real food and drink.

I can hear the words spoken aloud, even though I am reading silently. I realize that the energy coming through the text is a dear old friend, one whose voice I have not been able to hear in a very long time. This is so comforting that I decide to read aloud so that my own voice will merge with that of the book.

Hearing the sound of the two voices mingling together is like the harmony of water bubbling over rocks in a brook, or the sound of a symphony of birds calling forth the day. Reading in this way makes me breathe even more deeply , so I will proceed until I might be drawn back into the silence of reading and listening to this old friend speak alone.

I am sitting in the quiet of my study. The children are still asleep, and the book is open and cradled in my hands. The early morning sun is casting light through the eastern window and I can smell the calling of the lilac bush. As lovely as the day is, beckoning me to go work in the garden, I am compelled to listen to this book.

I am reading of a group of people who walked upon a dying planet in a timeless space, and all that they encountered along the way, in an effort to gather sunlight for their homeland. Their sun was beginning to die slowly and with signs that only a handful of people noticed. Those who were aware lived selflessly, enduring such trauma as they went about their mission, traveling throughout the land. They figured out a way to collect the light into their own bodies and spread it throughout all life on their planet. As these people worked to share this life-giving light, they came to realize that each additional person receiving it actually served to strengthen the energy of their own planet's sun.

These people are known to me. This work they did is real.

The frequencies of this book are moving into my bones. As strange as that sounds, it is the closest description to what is physically happening. This has got to be a direct connection to what happened last night.

Just yesterday, my spine and the muscles around it felt so heavy and weighted. I do an exercise class four times a week and am accustomed to the exertion, but yesterday I felt as if I had run a marathon. There was an unknown and unexplainable heaviness within my mind as well. I had no reason to feel this burden, and it was a sensation I wanted gone. My usual prayers and stillness were not doing the trick; I had needed something bigger.

Another lightning storm came through late in the evening, and I went outside to sit in the garden chair to watch it. I recalled how Mother H had come spiraling down in her gold and purple tornado-like appearance around this time last year, and I yearned to see that again, although I knew there could never be another experience just like that. It had been a most phenomenal moment.

I needed the visual medicine of those cracks of lightning in the distance, signs of Mother H's presence, to reach me somehow. I needed the tight sensation in my body to be lifted instantaneously by that light in the sky. At least, that was what I was hoping for. For in spite of many wondrous and glorious things that have occurred in these past few years since I moved back to my lovely Annica, there still seems to be something imprisoned in my flesh that I cannot release. It is old, but not as old as the source of that blessed lightning, to be sure.

The experience last night is definitely intertwined with what is happening now as I read this mysterious book. There is a link here, but I have to describe what happened in full before I continue to read ahead.

What I remember is that I was observing the sky as it changed from a deep sky blue to milky gray-blue and then to that in-between place where no part of the sky is a constant color, right before a storm. Off to the north, well beyond Annica land, I saw the first cracks of lightning rip through the sky, kissing the ground for a split second. I gasped with delight, and coinciding with those lightning strikes, I felt something in my spine pop, followed by an instant sensation of release.

"Oh, dear God, I want more of this," I thought. All day, my spine and the muscles around it had felt heavy, weighted down, and exercise offered no release. My mind, as well, felt heavy and sluggish, but I could identify no reason for it.

There was no more time for self-centeredness. The lightning was sending vibratory messages ripping through my body, clearly communicating the possibilities contained within The Great Plan. I opened my mouth, feeling as if my ears and mouth were connected. I wanted the whole of my body to inhale this inundation of words of healing and hope.

The jagged spears of lightning descended from the sky one after another. I felt them shoot through me, even though they were at a distance and posed no danger of electrocution.

I laughed. The trees, flowers, and plants of the Annica Gardens shook with delight, titillated by the joy of the moment. There was no significant wind, but the redbud trees all swayed in one direction, and the flowers in front of them all bowed and bobbed in the other. It was a strange display of fanciful expression on their part.

I stood up and curtsied to them all as the color beings of each plant and tree were excited into a rainbow fountain by the lightning storm. Tiny filaments of colored light exploded out of each blade of grass like mini geysers, blossoming into snowflake-like patterns as they touched the air, then floating off like little supernatural hot air balloons. Meanwhile, the tall trees waved their green-gold salutations to Mother H up and out and beyond. I felt I was being drawn in among them all to join in their dance. How glorious is this life.

It was then that I realized something wonderful about this lightning—the lightning itself was feeding energy and nourishment to all of life on Earth.

People tend to fear lightning. They get out of swimming pools, turn off computers, stay away from trees, and a number of other precautions when a big storm hits, and this may well be wise behavior. It became clear to me, however, that Mother H was using the lightning as a way of casting her supernatural love over all creatures, great and small, just as Annie does when she manifests the northern lights. If people of this planet need to awaken, then a loving jolt from Mother H certainly can't hurt.

Each time a lightning sword jabbed its way through the distant skies, the trees responded with a show of heightened vigor in their dance. The rainbow color beings of the garden also were also recharged, their vibrations energized to be launched forth from every purple clematis, yellow broccoli flower, orange iris and pink phlox. Even the low-lying lavender and rosemary plants straightened themselves up a little higher into the sky as Mother H's lightning bolts cracked down from the heavens.

Through the tumult of the storm, a song came to me and I sang it softly, making a point to remember it so that I could record it later. I was deeply affected by the experience and I wanted to stay in it forever, but I was burning with the need to fulfill the direction I had been given. I knew I needed to go back into the house and get to work on my part to further The Great Plan.

I don't remember doing anything that I had planned to do. All I remember is waking up, picking up the strange book, and reading what I have just described of the book itself.

What happened to that burst of creative spirit and direction I had last night? Maybe the recharge was too intense for my nervous system to handle and I was forced to sleep so I could absorb it more smoothly. For whatever reason, I am on fire with love for God. There is not a moment that goes by without my awareness and knowing of, or my devotion to, the Presence of God.

Thank you, Mother H, for sharing your display with me, you are indeed His wonderful messenger here on Earth.

ELISE EXPLAINS HOW TO LIVE A LIFE OF WORSHIP

Worship is defined in Webster's dictionary as the feeling or expression of reverence and adoration for, or offered to, a divine being or supernatural power. This implies that true worship entails merely the conscious giving of honor to some sort of deity or cosmic frequency. But there are two simple and majestic aspects of life's eternal reality that add significantly to the definition:

1. Only God controls all life.
2. All life is inter-connected and inseparable.

Because we each comprise a small part of God's life, we cannot exist in isolation from God's omnipresence. Worship is the means by which the grandeur of this impeccable relationship can be known, and its practice and activity becomes as simple as the next breath when loving God comes first in the personal life.

God's Presence is experienced through the activity of worship, which forms the bridge by which the inter-relatedness of all life is first understood, then more deeply experienced as the very essence of that which unifies all of humanity within eternal life.

We are already completely whole in the love of God, and that alone is the cornerstone of true worship. To know this truth and to accept it as the reality governing each person's life in its purest essence is to live in communion with Creator. Let this thought interfuse the fullness of *who* you are. It is for the good of all life that you take this first step. Worship is further elevated by envisioning the web of truth that connects all spirit beings and all life within the love of God. When these basic foundations of worship are combined and incorporated into the vibrational essence of a being, they become the substance and fuel of one's existence on Earth and healing can occur. Worship is that simple.

Humanity has never collectively understood nor practiced the powerful simplicity of true worship. The whole of the human species needs healing, and Mother H wants the residents of Earth to comprehend how essential worship is, not just for the correction and restoration of the balance of the Creation Frequency, but so that each being can have the opportunity to reclaim their own place within eternity as well.

Religious dogma, false-faced social and political structures, indifference, and the destructive forces of atheism have run rampant so that the attunement of the inter-connectivity of life has nearly been lost in this world. Mother H desires that the activities of Godly worship be shared so as to bring the corrective frequencies into the life of mankind. She considers the strictures and wrong thinking inherent in all man-made religions to be ignorance, and the rejection of God to be a deceit that must itself be rejected.

All worship is intended to give praise and glory to God. It is the giving of everything of one's personal life, to God. By telling and showing God, moment-by-moment, that one is aware of God's supreme majesty, while acknowledging that all life belongs to God exclusively, worship is embodied and one becomes a conduit for the supernatural. The activity of worship brings humility to the worshiper, yet paradoxically, the one who worships also gains awareness of the individualized greatness of belonging to God. It is a superb and natural state of living resulting from the simple acknowledgment that God's love is endless and fulfilling for all and throughout eternity.

Loving and living for God creates a natural state of peace, contentment, and bliss. These gifts are part of the inherent condition of all spirit beings in their purest form. A person who knows they are loved by God, and knows they are made of this love, naturally radiates this same energy in the way they think, and in the speech, actions, and deeds of daily life.

The natural activity of worship is inherently supernatural as well. Remember that the Creation Frequency, which cannot be seen with the naked eye, holds all of life together, on this planet and all throughout space. This is God's spider web of life, which creates and fills you, surrounds and protects you. It is the very web of life connecting you inseparably to all forms of life everywhere throughout the universe.

Imagine what happens to the pristine web of the Creation Frequency when one puts the thoughts of worship into one's daily life. The very thoughts of a single person who knows they are made of God's supernatural love immediately energizes the rays passing through the Creation Frequency. Those humble and pure thoughts help to bring aid in the form of healing to the Creation Frequency, thereby directly affecting all life on Earth as we know it. Whether or not these effects are sensed immediately, the unseen rays energized by worship rebound back into this physical realm. In practiced stillness and quietude, the effects are known by degree and over time.

Yet another powerful effect of worship is that real-time healing becomes available to everyone. All one need do is let go of the falsehoods learned in the past and replace the lies with eternal spiritual truths. All beings are entitled to this gift as individuals made in the image of God's thought. Worship is the muscle that all humans can use to return themselves to the ever-present, eternal and infinite realm of Creator's Glory. It is the destiny of each and every individual to live within a unified consciousness of life so as to first, experience this wondrous natural state of being, then to understand it, and finally, to *know* it. It is up to each individual to reconnect with the exactness of what worship feels like and to learn how to make it the cornerstone of living as a spirit being made by Creator.

Humans are not native to Earth and are not exclusively human. Rejoice in the knowledge that you are a spirit being living in a physical body. Worship creates of this human life and body the temple that Creator wants to inhabit. This again is the unified collective destiny of all mankind.

Humankind has difficulty accepting the truth that it belongs to God. If it were otherwise, there would be no suffering on this planet and no need for writing these books. There are millions of people who really believe that God does not even exist, and millions more who claim to know of God but have so much mental interference blocking their receptivity to Unconditional Love that it is impossible for them to truly perceive of themselves as an integral part of life itself.

For the person who is willing to believe that God exists, but has no idea how to control an ego that clouds the efforts of the spirit being, the act of worship is a struggle, if not impossible. The ego, in combination with the conscious mind, will repeatedly thwart all efforts toward healing, attempting to keep the self in the world's collective state of mental disconnection.

Practical methods for making a life of worship.

Think outside the box. Think diligently and devotedly beyond the circumstances of your daily life, and let your inner voice be one of support, telling you that you belong to God.

Be a loving warrior. Hold thoughts of the past at bay forcefully with the flame of your determination to live according to God's Will and not your own personal will.

The activities of devotional thinking outside the box are simple, but they must be practiced continuously for your entire life. As long as you remain in a body, you are subject to the weakness of attachment to ego and the ways of the disconnected collective mind. While you are in the world, you must work your hardest to live for that which is beyond the world.

Putting worship into practice is a fine art that weaves the awareness of goodness into daily life, and transfigures negativity as by infusing it with positive energy. This process not only provides spiritual nourishment to the Creation Frequency but makes of the human a whole spirit being in mind and body. By putting worship into practice, the individual discovers that each and every moment *becomes* worship, allowing the individual a glimpse of heaven on this planet. By making the body and mind a temple for God, God's highest thought for human beings can be made manifest.

The components of daily life provide fertile ground for the activity of worship. The elementals, who are so commonly taken for granted, are all composed of spirit beings working together to support life, and they await your communication. The stars, earth, air, water, fire, breath, all await acknowledgment in your worship of God. The spirit being of water whose droplets so graciously cleanse and comfort your flesh in a shower, await your thoughts of gratitude. Fill each morning shower with appreciation for water's grace and power and willingness to assist your life. That water has made itself willing to take all your skin's impurities, helping your body to bring forth its newly born epidermal cells. Go deeper, remembering that when you thank and bless the water that you bathe in, drink, and nourish your gardens with, you are also blessing and transforming the water of your physical body and every other body on this planet and beyond. You change the very molecular structure of water on Earth in how you think of and through it. As your physical body contains more water than anything else—well over fifty percent—the power of transformation at the cellular level alone is incredible.

Water is a cosmic being with a supernatural form that has descended and is manifested in the form we know on this planet. By honoring the living quality of the spirit being of water, we contribute to its proper flow of cosmic cycling throughout Earth and this physical dimension and beyond. The never-ending ebb and flow of this precious spirit liquid is a circuitry of life, and a carrier of messages throughout the Earth and beyond. Water has consciousness and is most certainly not just H_2O.

At the microcosmic level, when water is given blessings of unconditional love, your own place within God's love is also blessed.

Worship God in the way you choose your foods, how you prepare them, and how you eat them, and elevate your devotional behaviors with regard to nutritional consumption. Recognize that each food is a spirit being in and of itself, having come from some seed or animal that is also a part of the life force constantly streaming from the Creation Frequency. Each type of natural food is born of the original thought of Mother H, using cosmic material created by God to bring the plant or animal into being in its original form. The food we eat is light transformed into organic compounds, so transform your thought in appreciation and honor of God's life in this way.

Bless God for being the original Source of your food and ask for extra divine radiance to enter each morsel. Thank God for bringing you such daily nourishment. Worship with gratitude, while envisioning proper sustenance being received by all on this planet for the fulfillment of their own life missions. Remember, you are becoming a stronger temple for God's Will. To pay attention to physical health is to listen to the whole of life as it moves through your own flesh. This is a core practice of worship.

Take a moment to worship God in the sound of a child's laughter, the night breeze as it carries the song of spring peeper frogs, in the warmth of the summer sun on your flesh. Acknowledge the gift of the breath of life from the trees, season after season. Observe a spider's web and contemplate that its wispy and perfect home is the most specific three-dimensional representation of the cosmic and supernatural Creation Frequency. Say thank you to Grandmother Spider for her modeling of this cosmic Web, invisible to your human eyes.

Remember your ancestors, known and unknown, and acknowledge that their contract with God to come to Earth also included your placement here. Study the lands from which they came while holding the awareness that they, too, were not of this world. Acknowledge the fact that all of their positive thoughts, prayers, and work remain in the rock and soil of this planet and in the third-dimensional realm as a whole. The frequencies of their spirit beings are very much present in tangible ways, but it takes worship to attune to this. Raise the vibration of your thoughts to remember that it is impossible that they are not alive, and that the fruit of their own hearts resides in yours.

The tiniest of the tiny and the greatest of the great are to be included in your diverse and simple worship.

It is up to you to discover the myriad of ways to activate faithful worship.

The actions of worship are also needed so that the mundane negatives will be replaced by God's positives. The ego can imprison the mind to such an extent that the mind may tell you that you are incapable of worship, and incapable of knowing yourself as a part of God's eternal Web of Life and Love.

The key to worship is to choose those thoughts and activities which hold specific meaning in your life for counteracting a problematic thought and behavior. If you struggle with welcoming abundance into your personal life, recall the fact that your physical body is made of trillions of cells, which are actually comprised of star matter, filled richly with oxygen by the involuntary breath you are given naturally by God's Spirit. By thinking in this way with regularity, you will call attention to the richness of life in your body . This will astound the conscious mind, overcoming all past subconscious nonsense, and will access the super-conscious level of mind where your true self resides. Thinking in terms of *breathing cellular abundance* will also call forth a wealth of physical healing. Breath is one channel of healing by which the Spirit of God is made known to humankind, and giving attention to it enlivens the body. This is not a conjured visual meditation; it is worship work that reconnects the human, as a spirit being among other spirit beings, to God.

Some practical activities of worship that might transform thoughts of deficiency could include feeding the birds in your yard every morning so that beings other than yourself may be provided for, or simply giving a smile or word of kindness in situations where another is feeling a paucity of it. Where there is the appearance or illusion of insufficiency, fill it with something rich and providential.

There is abundance everywhere, but it takes activities such as these to counteract in thought and deed the negative frequencies that compose a mentality of lack. As basic and easy as these suggestions may seem, they are neither noticed nor practiced by the majority of humankind.

If you have been continuously and negatively judgmental of yourself or another individual, go out of your way to think and say the opposite of what you have been expressing. Where there is animosity or criticism, radiate a caring and open heart. As everyone has had the experience of being the victim of disconnected thinking by another and thus lead to display anger, coldness, or indifference, each person has also the capacity to see through, above, and beyond the display of emotional thinking by intending and expressing the positive alternative. Even if a person has never experienced goodness from another human being, that same person has felt the sun shine, breathed the air, and been nourished by water and food. The forces of nature offered to all who occupy a physical body, are the offerings of goodness. Be the radiance of nature by offering intentional thoughts, words, and actions born of goodness for the benefit of another.

If you find yourself constantly thinking with hatred or anger towards someone from your past who behaved wrongly towards you, tell yourself that you and that person are made of God's Love, in form and in essence. That is the initial step toward healing and forgiveness. By giving yourself and the wrongdoer the same loving energy that God gives to all beings, no matter what they have done, you instantly cleanse the negative. At the same time, you make room for God's presence to fill the void where the hurt had been. Take the first step of willing a loving thought to one who has caused harm, and God will always do the rest.

Forgiveness is one of the highest forms of worship, indeed, and it is also a supernatural tool that contributes to an immediate correction of damage to the Creation Frequency. When loving thoughts and behaviors are given with consistency, the holes torn in its radiant web by millennia of destructive emotional thoughts are healed instantly. Intentionally good thoughts are transmitted as energetic light, adding to the perfect functioning of the Creation Frequency.

Yet forgiveness is likely one of the most difficult forms of worship, as the emotional thinking of ego does not want you to forget suffering, especially when perceived as having been caused by another. Remember that ego is fed by negative emotional thinking, and ego fuels the greed of personal power. These are the two forces that Din identified as perpetrators of the unwillingness to change for the better. Of greater concern, they are also the energies by which life on Earth is being destroyed.

When millions of people have difficulty forgiving one another, they and millions more become a weakened species, easily controlled by even more negative forces contradictory to life itself.

Become a kind of warrior for worship. Challenge the conscious mind and ego in each and every emergent thought and eliminate those that do not serve the heart. The repetition of your worship activity is vital to overcoming the negative energy that has plagued the self and humanity for ages.

The point is to constantly counteract, in thought and deed, the mental energies that have hindered your growth or kept you stuck in a state of suffering. Interfuse into every moment, the confession of the goodness of all life.

When you are unable to see yourself as a reflection of God's love you cannot know yourself as inseparably linked to the lives of all others. No matter how many thoughts or activities you intentionally change, it is wise to acknowledge that the new behavior has been adopted not only to give yourself to God, but that it is done for the benefit of all beings and, most importantly, for the Praise and Glory of God.

Day by day, you will see that the tiniest thoughts and activities of goodness and worship lead to healing. Worship brings direct blessings to the one worshiping and to all beings, no matter what galaxy they live in.

Let the beautiful irony remain strong and clear: it is the simple and small that makes for the most powerful of God's manifestations in the realm of the third dimension.

With all of that in mind, let me offer a truer, yet simpler definition of worship:

> *Worship is the activity of reverence and adoration of God, which is communion in God, done intentionally for the benefit of all.*

***

"Okay, Mary, is there anything else that needs to be said about worship for now? I guess I could go more into a description of the Great Tree of Life and how true worship affects it. What do you think?"

Mary: *Dearest Elise, what you have done here is perfect for now. A description of the Great Tree will have to wait, and as patience is a virtue that must be acquired, we will provide yet another opportunity for all to worship in this way. You have also been writing for hours, so you must be off to sleep. And do not attempt to stay up for another hour in silence, or to "travel" as you like to describe it to Din. I tell you that you must go to sleep now, understood?*

"Yes, Mary. You are beginning to sound like Mother."

Yes, and I also sound like you when you talk to those children of yours who frolic about when they should be brushing their teeth at night.

"Okay, then, I am off to let the bedbugs bite. I have just one question, though."

Yes, Elise?

"I have been getting a strange feeling about something that is going to happen soon. We have a Gathering coming up, but something about it is bothering me and I can't put my finger on it. Will you give me any clues as to what's going on?"

Would you also like me to tell you the exact date of the end of The Great Plan as well?

"Ha ha. Nice one. I can see you've been practicing your sarcasm. I take it the answer is, no. You won't tell me anything, huh?"

Sweet dreams, Elise.

THE STRONG WEET MEET A CONTRARY VOICE

It has been customary since the release of *The Lost Revelation* for all the Strong Weet to come together for what Din had been calling a development circle. He had thought that the Strong Weet might need some refreshers, or possibly even activities new to their conscious minds, to aid them in achieving their personal awakenings to who they really are as beings from Hectarus. However, we all considered the "development" part of the designation to be irrelevant after our first meeting during which we experienced a supernatural surprise from Annie, and observed each other's strong and natural spiritual attunements, as detailed in *Volume Two*.

Immediately after the first development circle, the format of our meetings changed from highly structured, preplanned discussion and activity to meetings in which we found ourselves completely controlled by the Will of God's Spirit. We decided to simply acknowledge what was being done through us. As God was calling us to gather together in our frequencies, our hearts, and our minds, to be used as a microcosmic model of what is desired for the world, our weekly meetings have been renamed formally as Gatherings.

The events of one Gathering in particular took us all by surprise. Joyfully anticipating the meeting to come the next day at Merta's house, I went to sleep the night before dreaming of the scrumptious Mexican empanadas she had promised us.

Following my usual hour of silence the next morning, I checked my email, and was aghast to discover this one from Din:

29

> The plan for the Gathering has
> changed for today. Meet me at the
> McDonald's on Nifong. Have already
> talked with Merta and Sit.
> DO NOT BE LATE!
> I will have your Big Mac waiting for you.

"WHAT?" I rubbed my eyes in disbelief, a bit of shock, and a great deal of disgust.

I re-read the message twice, hoping it would somehow miraculously change.

My little dog, Opi, stared up at me as the image of a Big Mac entered our minds at the same time. His stumpy little tail wiggled with excitement, while all I could muster was disgust.

"Don't get too excited, Opi. There's no way in the world I'm going to eat that stuff. I wouldn't even feed it to you, my precious puppy."

Opi whimpered in disapproval of my conviction. Din always had a good reason for everything, and it was now fifteen minutes until our meeting time — and the Strong Weet are never late for anything.

I walked into the McDonald's and found Din, Merta, and Sit, already seated at one of those bolted down fast-food tables. They had apparently noticed my expression and were getting great enjoyment from it — Din especially. They all knew of my fastidious tastes when it came to health and diet. They laughed at me and I realized I had been set up.

"Ah, just in time for your super-sized fries, Elise," Din said, smirking.

"Gee, thanks. I really am excited about replacing Merta's homemade empanadas with McDonald's."

Din was itching for me to ask why, but I decided not

to grant him the pleasure. Instead, I widened my smile.

"I'm so very happy to see you all, as always." I took my seat, but not before making sure there wasn't anything nasty smeared on it. I had vivid memories of visits to fast food restaurants as a child and, more often than not, discovering wads of gum, streaks of grease, and sticky crumbs on the seats and undersides of tables

"Oh, relax, Elise, you know we were all drawn to come here because of the fries. You gotta admit, the fries are classically good," Sit said, with total sincerity.

"It's okay, *mi'jita*, I brought empanadas for all of us. I do not disappoint *mi familia*." Merta smiled while lifting four large, foil-wrapped, hot empanadas from her linen satchel.

Din said, "And what would accompany those lovely empanadas better than hot, steaming fries all around? I'll be right back." He was away quickly in order to get in line before a herd of Boy Scouts that had just trooped in.

"Okay, I am happy to see how content you all are to be here, and happier still that I get to eat one of these. Thank you, Merta, and praise God." I began to unwrap an empanada.

"What on Earth is there to praise God for? You must be in the wrong place, lady," said a gravelly female voice.

I looked up to see a woman with leathery skin that matched her gritty voice approach our table. She held a damp rag in one hand while attempting to pin her McDonald's cap more firmly to her hair with the other. She cleared her throat.

"I'm sorry," she said. "I don't mean to interrupt. I was actually coming over here 'cuz I realized that the table you all are at didn't get quite cleaned up after that other family was done usin' it just 'fore you came in."

Merta, Sit, and I glanced at one another.

"Feel free to do what you need," Sit said sweetly, "What's your name?"

"Cheryl."

"Nice to meet you, Cheryl."

Cheryl proceeded to wipe down the table, quickly and thoroughly.

"Sorry to bother you. Have a nice day." She started to walk away but stopped when Sit touched her arm lightly.

Sit looked at her kindly. "Well," she said, "I don't think you mean that. If you really meant what you said about having a nice day, then you would know what having a nice day feels like, and that's having something to praise God for, now isn't it?"

Cheryl seemed momentarily stunned. She recovered quickly and replied, "Lady, my life is hell. Always has been, always will be. I just get tired of hearing folks like you acting like it's all hunky dory. This world is messed up, and if you can't see that I think you better take stock of what world you think you're in."

Just then Din came back with a tray of four super-sized bags of hot fries. He smiled at the woman , put the tray on the table, and sat down saying, "Well, sorry it took so long. I convinced the guy up there to cook these with a fresh batch of oil. I wanted them to be just right. I haven't had these in years.

I closed my eyes and thought, *Why on Earth are we here, Mother?*

Eat the fries, Daughter.

Cheryl stood with her hand on her hip, looking uneasy. Din, Merta, Sit, and I kept our bags of fries on the tray, and began to dip into them. Properly chastened, I took one fry at a time and nibbled on it with great attention.

Memories of eating those crispy, salty, potato slivers when I was a child flooded my mind. I smiled as the image of my deceased father, Pacelli, brought sensations of tingling joy through my body. He had fallen into the practice of taking me to McDonald's every Wednesday evening, and buying me a happy meal, because he really thought it made me happy.

I licked the salt from my lips. "You know, memories are a funny thing," I said. "Everybody has them—the good, the not-so-good, and the in-between kind. It's the not-so-good ones that seem to plague the mind and keep people down. But none of that past is real. It came, it went, and it's now dead. It's the addiction to the memories that becomes real and can take over one's life." I looked at Cheryl, who was looking at me with a mixture of interest and scorn.

"Listen, lady, I clock out in twenty minutes, and in forty minutes I have to go pick up one of my kids from daycare, drop him off at his grandma's house, go beg my landlord to let me have another week to get the rent paid, go visit my other kid in jail, and then go off to my other crappy job. Since my husband left me after my third kid died a few years ago, this is the kind of life I've had. You talk about memories? Well mine are way beyond not-so-good. My memories are nothin' but pure pain."

Merta had been eating her empanada and fries, keeping her eyes downcast. It was a habit she had picked up from her own *abuela*—to never look directly into the eyes of anyone she did not know. The rest of us looked straight at Cheryl as she spoke. Suddenly Merta looked up at her with the most tender of gazes.

"I do not know you and you do not know me, *Señora*, but I am so sorry for your pain in the loss of your child. I, too, know what it is like to lose a child. Please know that I, a complete stranger to you, can take your pain away from you in the name of God, because it is my own as well."

We all felt the effect of Merta's utterance of the vibration of Unconditional Love wash through us. Cheryl's face softened, her tense shoulders unlocked, and she dropped her washrag. Tears welled up in her eyes, but she squeezed her eyes shut, willing them not to fall.

Cheryl stood speechless, clutching her belly as if someone had hit her hard. When she was able to speak, she said, "What just happened? How on Earth can you do that, ma'am? I mean, take away my pain. I know you all won't understand this, but the moment you said that, ma'am, about taking away my pain, I felt a knot that's been in my stomach for years just disappear."

Merta's smile grew wider. "It is the workings of The Lord, *Señora*. I know what it is to live a life free of my past because I gave everything to God after my son died. That is all I could do because the pain was unbearable."

"No, you don't get it. I had the knot for years, and three weeks ago, a doctor told me I had cancer. I'm telling you right now that same knot is just gone. There's no more pain in my stomach!".

"Praise God!" I said, perhaps a bit too loudly, as people at other tables turned to look at us.

"Indeed." Merta was shining, "I believe we have just witnessed a miracle pass through you, Cheryl."

"Well, you say that as if you are ordering a cup of coffee, like you see this kind of thing every day."

"Welcome to the reality of miracles, Cheryl. I hope you make good of it for the sake of others in your life," Din said after wiping salty oil from his lips.

"I don't know what you are talking about. Yeah, whatever happened just now felt real good, but I know my crappy life is still waiting for me. Pain won't disappear from my life just like that. Lady, I got a question for you, though." She looked at Merta who had taken a bite of her empanada.

"*Sí?*"

"How did you get rid of the bad feelings after your son died?" Cheryl asked earnestly.

Merta wiped a crumb from the side of her mouth and replied, "I would not allow those thoughts to control me. I knew none of those emotions were who I am. I had to give it away to God, each and every time another difficult one came through, and it became simple because I decided to believe that it was gone from me, that it had been permanently removed from my mind."

"So, you got saved by giving away your thoughts to God? Is that what you are telling me?" Cheryl's doubt was obvious.

Merta said, "I was saved from my own thinking, and yes, I was saved by God. There is nothing else that can heal the kind of pain and suffering that you, I, and all people know."

"But you just said before that you can take away my pain. Are you calling yourself God?" The colors around Cheryl's head were getting darker and darker. Merta was smiling but looked as if she was tired of talking.

I ate the last of my french fry and stepped in, "No, Cheryl, she is not calling herself God. She is sharing with you the truth of what pure love can do. When just one person lives a life that is fully devoted to love, then pain is eradicated, and that one person has the power to take pain away from another, in the name of this kind of pure Love, which is God. It does not take long at all to be healed if you would just give it all away to God. We are all made of this very same love, Cheryl."

"I've been giving myself away my whole life. I don't think that's gonna work for me. I'm too stuck in what I have to do for everyone else." Cheryl's body tightened again, as she cleared her throat. "I gotta go now. It was sure nice talkin' to you all, whoever you are."

"Cheryl, one last thing before you leave," I said.

She looked at me with tired eyes.

"Thank you for being here. It has been such a blessing to meet you."

"No one has ever said that to me, ever." Cheryl's hands were shaking as she stuffed them into her pockets. "I don't know what to make of you all, but uh, you are welcome, I guess."

"Well, I guess we're done here," Din said, smiling radiantly. "Anybody wanna pick up another bag of fries before we all go our separate ways? It's on me."

We laughed as we gathered our belongings and walked out of McDonald's, full of the nourishment of joy. It had been a most unexpected experience, and a pure transmission of Unconditional Love. But in all truth, isn't that what daily life is filled with anyway?

It is distressing to observe how so many people on this sacred and life-giving planet are filled with an addiction to the past, pain, and even death.

THE ADDICTION TO DEATH AND THE EXPRESSION OF LIFE

Humanity is all too familiar with the process of physical death, resulting in a disconnected culture that expects it and is accustomed to it. Because physical death is considered to be a finite and unavoidable reality of the human experience, the collective human mind has integrated it as a part of the excessively ego-ridden human drama on Earth.

The range of obsession with death culture can be seen as a spectrum with, for example, drugs to ward off death at one end, and the billion-dollar industry of Hollywood violent movies at the other. Twenty-first century humanity fears the reality of the body breaking down, but at the same time loves to be titillated by the thrill of destruction on the big screen. To know what lies in the middle of the death culture spectrum, turn on the daily news and observe the manifestations of addiction to life versus death drama, with billions of people acting the starring role.

MARY: *It is disconnected thinking that keeps the whole of mankind at a distance from living within God, Elise, and humanity must understand how simple it is to correct this!*

Absolutely, Mary. There is great medicine in just one more person choosing to reconnect with Truth and Unconditional Love. Life is life is Life. Do you want to take over here?

No, you are doing a fine job. Annie will be here soon. Continue.

It is this death awareness that, in part, makes the concept of "living for the Now" so attractive to the disconnected and spiritually hungry. There is a spectrum of chaos with the mindset of self-serving existence on one end, and living thoughtlessly in the present moment and with no real honoring of God, on the other.

Certainly, if one's reality contends that the observable, material, physical life is all there is, with nothing conclusive and provable by science to follow, then one is going to want to make the present reality as fulfilling, and as free of pain as possible. It's as if the phrase, *carpe diem*, which is meant to inspire one to live true life to the fullest, becomes, *Get what you can, while you can, cheaply, and now.* Daily living becomes the quest to take actions that are only for the self and one's immediate dependent family. Seeing the world from a strictly material point of view excludes the eternal reality of life's intertwining, inter-related nature—the butterfly effect—that reveals that all thought and activity directly affect everything else in life.

Man's world of infatuation with the material cannot be a world where to *do unto others as you would have another do unto you* is primary. The stock market does not rise and politicians do not stay in power by way of a system that loves God first and loves one's neighbor as one's self.

What then of the feel-good industry of living in the now, which speaks nothing of God's power but focuses on recreating a new planet by way of self-empowerment and ridding the mind of ego-based living? Surely, the latter is necessary to reconnect oneself with the enormity of everlasting life, but at this end of the material-minded spectrum, there still remains observable disconnection.

Yes, God wants all people to live in peace within an eternal moment of now, where no images of the past control any aspect of that present moment. But one cannot accomplish anything for the self or the world without the Presence of God, and where there is no recognition of God, the activity of living for the now is incomplete and ineffective. To say that human beings can do anything good by personal will alone is not just incorrect; it is impossible.

If a book intended to provide spiritual insight makes no mention of God being the Ultimate Power behind every aspect of life on Earth and instructs the reader in meditation techniques without acknowledging that the purpose for the exercise is to honor and connect more deeply with God, then the text is useless for the purposes of receiving life beyond the third dimension.

The highly marketable mindset, which supports the contrived notion that life is distant or even separate from God, is no accident, by any means.

The material mind feeds the addiction to the physical, and vice versa, which then becomes the hologram of reality for a culture. It is a dangerous mentality of disposable objects and diseased bodies, the inevitable end of which is physical death.

In the material mind of physical addiction, the human body becomes victim as well. An example of the thinking displayed in this form of disconnection would be: Well, everyone is born with their own set of good genes or inherited problems. It's just nature. If you get sick, go to a doctor. They are finding cures for major diseases all the time, so maybe, if you have the insurance, you can get the drugs you need to help you get through it. There is probably a surgery that can take care of that particular problem.

The imprisoning belief that many people have integrated as reality is that intense bodily conditions are of a permanent nature and completely irreversible. This is a dangerous lie that must be seen through and challenged by the person who is ready to embrace the promises of God, who has clearly stated that all iniquities and diseases have already been lifted by God, the only requirement is that the individual believe that God is in complete control of all aspects of the life.

Believing that the body exists in isolation as flesh and is subject to the rules of the material and human physiology alone is another symptom of present-day disconnected cultural thinking. This has contributed to the manifestation of rampant commercialism, health care industries, medical institutions which support disease and death, and financial imprisonment, to name a few of the social ills that sever one's knowing of themselves as a spirit being.

Where, in such bondage of a material mind, is there the space for miracles of healing to be accepted as commonplace and even expected? For the multitudes of people on this planet who have become severed from the infinite reality of God's healing, there is little room in the conscious material-physical mind to accept these miracles.

ANNIE: *Good morning, Mother, Elise.*

Good morning, Annie. We've been expecting you.

MARY: *Good morning, Daughter. Annie, I would like you to explain a little more about the Family Triad and how we relate to Mother H and the work she is doing on this planet.*

ANNIE: *I would be glad to, Mother.*

First of all, I am the result of the miracle of the union of my mother and father, who are directly born of Mother H, who is directly born of God. Mother H assigned my mother, Mary, to implement and supervise her work on this planet. A primary task in these last remaining years is the transcription of her voice into the VOLUMES *of her* DIARY. *When I say "her voice" you must understand that Mary's voice is practically the same as Mother H's. Their union is like no other, and it could very well be said that* VOLUME THREE *is the culmination of the massive work that Mary has done for Mother H on this plane, for millions of years now. Father's part is to dispense instruction and to warn of discipline and judgment, but only Mary has direct charge of how all life is manifested in this particular universe.*

MARY: *Elise is correct in her assessment of the serious mental addictions that plague the people of this planet, the destructive behaviors that are the consequence. I have watched many residents of Earth choose to align themselves with the negative impulses and forces born of these mental choices.*

On a lighter note, I have been planning a gift for those who are choosing to follow the guidelines of the Weet. It is an energy current of a specific healing frequency that was established in the writing of VOLUME TWO *and strengthened when the book became available to the world. I smile in wonder and expectation, as I watch those on Earth who are willing to accept this all-powerful ray from God at the moment of its release. I have put great effort into the preparation and blessing of this cosmic gift for those who are serious about living as spirit beings for the good of The Great Plan. Those who have chosen to be such, grow increasing more aware of how their lives have been healed. In the lives of those secondary and support Weet who have been Awakened in the last few years, there have been many miraculous healings, as well as life-changing experiences.*

VOLUME TWO *was perfectly born and has taken root throughout this part of the Milky Way Galaxy.* VOLUME THREE *is empowering me to be returned to this dimension in the fullness of who I am.*

All that Annie has just said concerning our origins and mission is true. I am here now to relate further details and explain how they relate to healing.

First, the nature of who I am is inseparable from Creator's Healing frequencies. Each and every aspect of my being is the result of the communion of myself, Annie, Din, Mother H, and God. Throughout the four million years of my existence as an individual on this planet and beyond, I have been engaged in the activity of seeding and raising that which is pure in life. Before the thought of Mother H brought me forth into this form, I was infused with the purity of her force. She knew me to be the one who would do her work here and in a multitude of other star systems. I emerged from Mother H fully aware of my essence and ready to be trained for the divine work I was assigned to do, for Earth and beyond.

Simply stated, as regards my voice within the pages of this book, Mother H and I speak as one. Din has said that I speak in ways many people find difficult to understand and requests that I try to use modern Earth phrases. With that in mind, I say to you that Mother H and I are joined at the hip. Like Mother H, I am literally everywhere, in all moments, in each and every frequency of Creator's space, and when Elise writes of the healing, you can be assured that I am instructing every word.

Humanity needs to be aware that the subject matter of BEYOND INFINITE HEALING *is not only* A PROMISE FROM ABOVE — *specifically from myself and Mother H—but is also the everlasting reality of which human beings have at present no complete knowledge. Mankind has devolved into a carbon-bound species limited to three dimensions and is now physically dying; this being the result of choosing for millennia the thoughts and activities leading to the disconnection from the limitlessness of Creator's Love, which is eternal Life. You are truly free when you live in this way, and you will be a slave to nothing and no one.*

This volume of THE DIARY *is not only a gift that will heal, but it provides the key to living even beyond infinity. At this point in human development, the collective human mind cannot comprehend the enormity of what I am expressing, but that is why Din and Elise are writing this book. God has always wanted humanity to practice, understand, and know the Presence of God at all times. Many of the current philosophies are missing this point, and they do so intentionally because they have turned away from God and seek to assume that title for themselves.*

Choosing to live in the truth of a proper relationship with the true God—to live as children of God—is the path to true Healing.

Annie, do you wish to add anything?

ANNIE: *No, Mother. You stated it perfectly.*

MARY: *Elise, another simple, yet profound occurrence of a true miracle has come to my mind. I think you are most suited to relate the story.*

"Which one would that be?" I ask. "I could write for the rest of this lifetime about all the miraculous occurrences involving the Weet."

No answer.

WISDOM FROM THE WINGED ONES

I was deep in thought about this latest assignment from Mary as I walked to the kitchen. When I had refilled the mason jar I use for drinking with nettle and raspberry tea, I paused to look out the window, hoping for inspiration. There in front of me was a cardinal, just inches away. It was acting like a hummingbird, hovering in flight on the other side of the glass. For a moment, I thought the handsome red bird wanted to come into the house, but then I remembered something wonderful. The visitation from this dear friend made it clear that I am to relate the story of the bird who died and was saved one day last year. Thank you, little one.

It happened just before an exercise class. Din and I had arrived early, as usual, on a Friday morning, and were conversing while we prepared for class. The rented room for our weekly Gathering is large and comfortably carpeted, with floor-to-ceiling windows on the east and west sides. The early morning sunlight was streaming through the eastern glass panes, and I had walked over to observe the light merging with the waterfall upon the rocks, immediately outside. Being still while watching the light on the glistening rocks, is part of my usual preparation for and welcoming of the sacred energy of our weekly exercise.

Din broke the silence. "I am concerned about Merta. As one of our Strong Weet, it is not good that we haven't heard from her." He was seated at the opposite end of the room on the western windowsill, elbows resting on both knees with his chin perched on folded hands.

"She was fine when we all met for the Gathering a few weeks back, but she hasn't called or written us in days, and I don't like it."

Before turning away from the window, I blew a kiss to the quietude, the sunlight, the water, and the rocks, then I walked over to my exercise mat. I plopped down on it and looked up at Din. "She is fine. She's still grieving the passing of her son, Marcos. We've seen her express the ups and downs of her healing from his death, and some days of non-communication are to be expected. She will find us when she is ready, as she has been doing. Let it be for now."

It had been some many months since we received the sorrowful news of Marcos's passing in a car accident caused by a drunk driver who, by the way, had walked away from the scene unscathed. It happened not long after Merta's spiritual awakening to her true nature as a Hectaran Weet, and the news of his death shocked her and briefly filled her mind with deep sorrow. She had been doing a tremendous work of healing from the passing of a loved one, giving even more of herself to others than she had before. We all had seen her in various aspects of this timeless work and had prayed for her with attention and focus. When a person is consumed by death, chronic disease in oneself or a family member, or any other life disaster, there is always the danger that the human emotions accompanying those situations will entrap a person, Weet or not. Being stuck in emotion is the biggest detriment to any individual's progress in living as a spirit being, and we had been diligent in our efforts to support Merta so this would not occur in her life.

I focused my eyes on the horizon beyond the western windowpanes. The interplay of light is different on the west side where the sun's rays are intercepted by the mass of the building. The willow tree stood tall, waving its greeting toward the freshness of that October morning, and the differing shades of greens melted into the yellow-browns of the sleeping grasses. It had been an uncommonly warm autumn.

"The passing of Marcos is bringing about such healing for Merta, Din, and this is the force and faith by which we must hold her now. His choice to leave so abruptly was the catalyst that brought about her self-realization as a Strong Weet. She knows this. Her grieving is being transfigured into something greater, and she is aware of this mystery and riding with the tides as they come. I know she is well."

The sunlight became stronger through the eastern window, and a broad band of sun's ray flashed across the room, briefly connecting the sparkling waterfall on one side with the dancing willow tree on the other side of the building. As soon as the water, the room, and the tree were united by it, the light was gone. All things returned to their mundane, solid appearance. I continued to gaze out the western window.

"We bear witness to what the healing is, Din."

As the hard-consonant of Din's name left my tongue, a bone-crushing thud sounded from the window in front of me. A bird had crashed into the window, leaving its dusty imprint on the glass before falling to the ground below.

"Oh, sweet Jesus!"

Din turned in alarm. Together, we ran out the door and around the side of the building to get to the winged one. I squatted to look and saw that its neck had broken—its head hung at an awkward angle from the rest of its body, and it was not breathing. The glaze of death was turning its eyes from shiny black to dull grey as we watched.

Din and I were speechless, but from within our quietude we simultaneously offered the same prayer:

Precious Creator, heal this one by relieving it of its suffering. If it be Your Will to take this one, then so be it.

If it be Your Will to heal this one, then so be it. We claim Thy healing now.

We watched as the Glow of the bird waned, it's heartbeat ceased, and it's breath went still.

I focused my unblinking gaze on the neck of the bird.

Redeeming miracles happen outside of time, yet there we were, marking the passage of it as we watched this mystery unfold. Minutes passed as time seemed to stop in those moments, with the presence of myself and Din completely merged with this one bird, on the edge of mystery.

"Thank You, God. Your Healing is done."

At that exact moment God showed us His decision with the manifestation of a miracle. The severe angle of the bird's fractured neck begin to straighten. Ever so slowly, the distorted bulge softened and set back into the normal shape of a bird's neck.

Din stood watching attentively while I hovered over the bird. "Her Glow is changing, Elise. It's merging into green again."

I held my hands extended over the tiny creature's body, and I could feel and see the transition flow around and through its flesh. The sphere of this bird's life Glow was beginning to widen again, and the spirit of joy was overtaking the whole scene.

The bird still lying on the ground, began to move its head left to right and I began to hum a thread of melody, fainter than the sound of a bird landing on a branch. Its wings quivered as the healing ray washed through its body. The miracle of this resurrection grew and the bird hopped to its feet.

"Praises. Look, Din." The two of us were still tightly locked in our physical positions. I exhaled deeply welcoming the relaxation of my own back and the great peace of the moment.

"She isn't out of the woods yet," Din said. "She still can't fly but see if she'll hop onto your hand." His other-worldly focus and concentration within the healing put a look on his face that would scare most people.

I extended my left hand slowly, palm up and close to the ground in front of the bird. Without hesitation it hopped onto the center of my palm and looked up into my eyes.

"Okay, Precious, claim your healing. Fly!" I accompanied my words with a gentle uplift of my hand, but the bird would not fly. It remained nestled in my palm, gazing up at me.

"Well, let it be, Elise. Listen to your own words If you are telling me to relax about Merta, then you need to wait for this bird to be ready. The poor thing had a broken neck and just came back from the dead," Din said, shaking his head.

There was a clump of trees several feet from the building that offered shelter, so I carried the bird over to it. The bird seemed happier for this relocation yet remained stationary in my hand. I stroked its silky feathered back and kissed the top of its head. There was a part of me that wanted this bird to remain by my side forever.

"And so it is," Din said.

I gave it one more kiss, then smiling with gratitude I commanded, "Claim your healing, precious. Fly!"

With that, the redeemed bird fluttered up and landed on one of the lower branches of a giant oak. It turned toward us and trilled a pristine and perfect song of thanks and flew away.

We reflected and wondered for weeks about the bird and its resurrection, and it became a subject for shared contemplation at a Gathering of the Strong Weet. There was a collective sense of appreciation from Sit and Merta, when the details of the story were related to them. In fact, it was the news of the bird that brought Merta back into the flow of the Gatherings.

***

Two weeks after the incident, Merta and I were sitting in my living room. Merta was looking out the southern window, gently fingering the leaves of a baby basil plant. She said, "Elise, I have been thinking about that bird that is now flying off somewhere in its own heaven, now that it has seen death. Do you believe that your faith and Din's faith in God was the fuel for welcoming this particular miracle?"

"Yes, one part of faith is the belief in the aspects of God which are unseen. There is no faith without action. I act on faith that God is always in control, when physical circumstances look bleak, and time after time, I have witnessed miracles of many different kinds happen in God's name."

Merta picked a tiny leaf of the basil plant and ate it, and then said, "Well I am thinking now about my whole lifetime of faith in God—how I have always believed that physical death was nothing. When my son died in that horrible car accident, my heart was torn. He was a wonderful young man of unquestionable faith in God. I did not understand how something so horrible could happen to such a perfect lamb."

I looked up from my crochet work to face Merta directly. "Well, you had many months of mental hardship and grieving over the loss of Marcos. We all remember that. It was painful to feel your grief. But throughout all of it, you were also able to understand part of why Marcos had left this life, yes?"

"*Si*, of course. In the depths of my despair, I remind myself over and over of the fact that my Marcos left so that I would awaken *mas rapido* as the Strong Weet that I am. It was not something that I came to understand of my own, however. It was Din who explained this to me. I had to experience the truth of Marcos' great sacrifice on my own, so that the healing would be complete for me.

"At first, I wanted so badly to see my son magically come back to me, in his body. It was too much to have him gone. But as time passed, I came to embrace the beauty of what he had done for me. The more I stayed with this gift, the stronger I became in mind and body. Pacha Mama, *mi abuela*—my grandmother—became so much more important to me in those moments of deep despair, as all the ancestors should be for everyone. The most important lesson I learned is that miracles of healing are everywhere—and those of the physical are the least of them."

A Visit to Monk's Mound

Over the past year and a half, Din and I have added a few field trips into the flow of our Gatherings, which had at first been at one of our houses. The nature of Spirit coursing through each of them was exciting, energizing, and fulfilling.

It was great fun to recognize that we hold very little control over the Gatherings. There is no conjuring of anything, or summoning of entities with rites, incantations, or spells. We have never gathered to share personal totems, talismans, or outlandish ideas on how to attain a new level of magic or power. From the moment we began until now, we have gathered for one reason, for the promotion of the work of God within The Great Plan.

As related in *The Lost Revelation*, Merta and Sit had already shown their degree of awareness regarding their natures as spirit beings. From that first powerful Gathering and onward, the individual and collective level of the use of Creator's gifts through us was truly profound, but we were simply showing up to help direct the particular frequencies given by Mary, Annie, and Mother H. We needed some outings to really explore the scope of the gifts. We have done a number of really fun things together since the emergence of *The Lost Revelation*, all of them enriching and full of surprises that ricocheted out and well beyond our own daily lives. One of those trips proved to be quite providential, as well as miraculous.

***

It was a beautiful Spring day when I guided our little group on a mystery tour to visit the Cahokia Mounds Historic Site — specifically, to what has come to be known as Monk's Mound — in Illinois, east of St. Louis. The city had been laid out over a thousand years ago by the ancestors to serve as a center for trade, agriculture, and—most importantly—religious observance for the people up and down the Mississippi Valley and along its tributaries. The civilization was at its peak around the years 1050 to 1100, yet by the year 1350, the city was abandoned.

Monk's Mound is so-named because in 1809, a group of Trappist monks established a community there for a short time and used the terraces of the mound to grow their gardens safely above flood level. While the base of the mound occupies an area equal to that of the Great Pyramid of Giza, its height is truncated at about one hundred feet, providing ample space for the temples and dwellings of the Sun Chief and the other high priests at the top. It was the daily activity of worship that focused the Energy of the Creation Frequency and caused it to be collected and stored in the mound, and it was the release of that Energy that my daughter and I witnessed a year ago as I described in *Volume Two* of the *Diary*.

The geyser-like explosion of energetic cosmic Color Beings from the top of Monk's Mound that spring afternoon has settled down into a strong flow, cascading down the side of the mound to spread across the countryside. That display is not readily visible to ordinary human eyes, but Din and I were confident that Sit and Merta had the ability to see it and we wanted to observe their responses to the energy of the holy grounds. The activation of Monk's Mound was contributing greatly to counteract the negativity plaguing the body of Earth, but the reason for our visit to that powerful place was for a more specific healing purpose.

I had kept our destination a secret from everyone, including Din, which gave a sense of intrigue and suspense to our two-hour car ride. I asked Merta and Sit if they would like to be blindfolded for the last thirty miles so that they might be able focus their spirit senses on the energies as we approached our destination and use the exercise to strengthen their own attunement.

Din had already figured out where we were going, and he smiled his approval when I presented the opportunity for spirit-mind exercise.

"Yes, I will do this," Merta said, "as long as you are not taking us to another cave. I liked that one where we could all see each other's Glow while sitting in the dark womb of the cave, but I would prefer to also be able to see with my two eyes, Elise, in case I were to fall into the water again by Abuela's doing." We all chuckled, remembering Merta's tale of her sort-of forced baptism on the banks of Stephens Lake when Merta's grandmother came to her from another realm.

"I want to be blind-folded, too," Sit said. "I can't wait to really see what's behind of all this!"

We pulled into a rest area where we tied blue bandannas over their eyes. The two women stayed quiet for the last thirty miles, concentrating on what their spirit eyes were "seeing", and anticipating what awaited us at our destination.

I asked Din to take the wheel when we were ready to continue because I could feel the Creation Frequency vibrate through my body with increasing force and I wanted to concentrate solely on that. I became the spirit of quiet as well, so that Merta and Sit would be unaffected by either Din or me.

I had carefully planned our trip to Monk's Mound to coincide with time and day of the week when it would be the least crowded as I wanted to insure a quiet atmosphere while we communed with the energy there. My efforts were rewarded and there was no one else at the

Mound but us.

Din parked the car and we all got out, then we guided Sit and Merta, still blindfolded, to the base of the Mound.

"What, if anything, do you notice?" Din asked.

The two women stood still and silent for about seven minutes before either of them reacted. Merta spoke first with great excitement, "I have never seen Grandmother take on so many different and beautiful colors! At first *mi abuela*, Maria, appeared to me as usual, but as we got closer to wherever we are, she exploded herself into trillions of these … these … bands of light rising into the sky."

"There is a pattern like a network," Sit added. "A grid of brilliant crystal energy. I'm not seeing streaming colors, but I am seeing an awesome, perfect web of light that's not color—or at least not any I have ever seen. It's impossible to describe."

Merta continued, "There are many, many ancestors here, and they are very happy to see us. There is a big party going on, and I think we are invited."

"There is something coming out of the grid now," Sit announced. The part of her face not hidden by the bandanna was suffused with joy. "No, wait—the grid is getting wider. It's growing. Wow, it got even bigger right after I said that. We are a part of this grid, wherever we may be, but the power is especially strong here in this place. I am so thankful to be here!"

The energies of Merta and Sit's wonder and excitement intertwined with each other, expanded, and soon began to combine with the colors and light emanating from the mound. The upward stream became swirls of geometric patterns, coming together in a shape like an infinity symbol or a Möbius strip. The entire grid was expanding with the thoughts of the two Strong Weet like a giant cosmic balloon, filling the space for hundreds of feet around.

This was what was visible to my eyes, and I suspected that Din was seeing the same thing.

"Glorious. Keep watching, ladies," I told them.

Sit and Merta remained blindfolded and in their positions. I asked them to squat down and place their palms on the grassy spot where the flatness of the Earth met the rise of the ancient prayer spot.

"There is indeed a party going on," I said, "and our arrival is the reason for the Gathering. Ladies, may I touch the back of your necks, where your head meets the spine? Din, I think it's time."

"If you all are ready." Din stood to my right, observing the supernatural wonderland of perfected Color Beings streaming out of Monk's Mound as they rose and descended and rose again within the rounded web of the Creation Frequency. The whole of the Color Beings within the Creation Frequency, the ancestors, and all of our thoughts were holding the Earth in that moment. In an ancient and timeless way, this experience was affecting all of life in a most profound way.

Din's eyes were on fire like a pair of golden phoenixes, and his smile added to the perfection of the moment.

Merta and Sit consented to my touch. I squatted between them, closed my eyes, and used the tip of a finger to gently locate the energetic center at the base of each woman's skull. I paused for a moment, listening for my cue. I found my beat and joined in with the Hum.

Merta and Sit became engulfed in the stream of shooting Color Beings. Their own energies reached out to join with it, causing their bodies to vibrate gently. At some point they had both shifted out of their squats and were now seated firmly on the sacred ground. Their inhales deepened as the cosmic gift from Creator's hand moved through them.

The web of the Creation Frequency—the grid described by Sit—reverberated with the harmonics of the cosmic orchestra of the spirits of Peace, Joy, Harmony, and unconditional Love, saturating us all with these gifts.

People of Earth tend to think of these four spiritual gifts as feelings or conditions of mind. They are in reality living spirits and aspects of God, and do not emanate from the minds of humans. In that moment at the base of Monk's Mound, they were merging with the most perfected of the Spirit Beings and blending with our DNA, and because of our willful communion with them being amplified throughout the planet, there at Monk's Mound. Our individual and shared level of practiced devotion to God was the reason for this symphony of heaven on Earth. What came next however, was as sweet as Life itself.

You are the blessed gifting of my heart.
Take me and spread me through all that you think,
all that you say,
and all that you do.
Your work is precious to me.

There she was, Mother H, towering over us in her personification as the Divine Mother. She filled the sky, and from our point of view appeared to be standing on Monk's Mound, with her great toe covering the whole of the top of it. She took up the threads of the energy grid and gathered them to her, absorbing them into her presence. She herself became the central fountain spewing forth the waves of Color Beings, the grid becoming all her own. She leaned down through time and space so that her face took the position where her toe had been at the top of the mound. As she did, the sun in Earth's sky was subsumed by her Glow and added to the illuminating radiance of her essence. Her light was blinding, yet we were still able to see.

We were tiny, but huge within her eternal and unassailable Glow. We melted into her all-consuming love, and there was no such thing as body, mind, or individual spirit. There was only God at work through Mother H.

Mother H's expression was translated into the center of each of us. The cells of our bodies hummed with the clarity of her words, and for that moment, the interfusion was complete within us. Most importantly, she had rooted us more deeply in infinity in order to accomplish all the work we must do on Earth in the coming years.

She winked at us, and it all disappeared—the light, the grid, the Hum—leaving nothing but total darkness and silence for the bare second that her eye was closed. Her eye opened, the world returned, and then she was gone.

***

The four of us were left standing in that sacred, although now perfectly ordinary spot on a now perfectly ordinary spring afternoon. In spite of the apparent mundanity of our surroundings, we could all sense a lingering vibration, like a great bell had been struck and the immense tone has faded beyond hearing but can still be felt deep in one's bones. The Great Plan was resonating with a degree of supernatural energy never before known on this planet. We knew that God's Will through us and the nature of our thoughts had brought about a change for Earth. We also knew that the world at large would not see, let alone understand the import of what had just happened. Mother H's gift was being felt by the Earth and all the heavens, and would continue to be manifested in the ongoing processes of destruction and creation that comprise but the tiniest wisp of her hair, blowing in the winds of the cosmos.

We were once again reminded of and impressed with how important every thought, word, and action by every human being is to the outcome of The Great Plan. The words of Mary's warning are about to be fulfilled. The rhythm of the ticking of Earth's clock has shifted into double time.

THE FOURTH STRONG WEET

The visit to Monk's Mound and the ancestors left us with feelings of ecstasy—and of great hunger. It had been an inter-dimensional, timeless immersion, drawing on the very life force of our beings. Apparently, Mother H needed a lot of our physical energy as well as her own in order to do what she had just done for all of us.

We still had not ascended the steps of Monk's Mound, and I suggested that we bypass that activity, given the enormity of what we had just experienced, and instead go get some dinner.

I had grown up around here, and so knew of many good places to go for food. I would have suggested my favorite Thai restaurant or perhaps a truly lovely Indian buffet, but I was drawn instead to a place I normally would not have chosen.

"So, do you all trust me enough to let me guide you to a place to eat?" I asked.

Din looked at me with mock suspicion. "Yes, as long as you don't take us to a place that serves sautéed tree roots and weeds for its main entrées. I need hearty options, Elise."

"After all we just experienced, I really don't care where we go, just as long as the food is good." Sit was always up for adventure and trying new things.

"I do not know this city at all, Elise. My only hope is that you do not choose Mexican, for obvious reasons." Merta's years of cooking, learned from her *abuela* and practiced from a young age, had made her the authority on this planet for perfect Mexican food. She was offended by the lack of authenticity and sub-standard dishes prepared by most Mexican restaurants in this part of the country.

"Well then, follow me." We all hopped into the car, and

I drove us to the place Mother H was prompting me to go.

I no longer question Mother H's direct commands, having learned to distinguish between what is coming from her mind and what is coming from my own consciousness. It used to be that I'd have to ponder the two in order to decide which was which, but now there is very little difference between my own will and hers. I heed what comes through my mind as coming from her wisdom and direct guidance.

We proceeded to a busy section of St. Louis—a popular commercial district considered by the local folk to be culturally hip. The eating establishments of that district offer a variety of interesting and diverse global cuisine. I was taking us to one that served Italian food. Din was going to be pleased, as he has an insatiable appetite for good Italian food, which, he claims is difficult to find outside the larger cities.

We approached the busy restaurant just as a car was vacating a parking spot right in front of it. I pulled in and we all got out. I was ready with the change for the meter when I saw that it still had a full hour and a half before expiring. I stared at the paid-up meter with its green band and descending numerals of digital minutes and offered a silent prayer of thanks, *You are always providing, Holy One, always.*

We stepped across the concrete sidewalk to the restaurant, unaware of what Mother H had prepared for us inside this place, in joyful anticipation of what I knew would be ceaseless abundance streaming our way. As Din opened the door, our nostrils were filled with the escaping aromas of bread and Italian herbs, causing our mouths to water.

The place looked as if it had been airlifted from somewhere out of southern Italy and dropped into the middle of Saint Louis, Missouri. The music of Louis Prima played in the background, mixing well with the friendly chatter of the patrons in the restaurant. The atmosphere was lively, but not loud. We could hear the stern but jovial-sounding head chef barking out orders to the lesser cooks, and from somewhere in the distance came the sound of bubbling water. Two large potted palm trees stood stoically, one on each side of the door, to greet the arriving diners.

It happened the moment my body entered the foyer. My vision went galactic, yet I remained aware of everything and everyone contained by the three-dimensional space of the restaurant.

I saw color beings of all hues dancing in strange and wondrous kaleidoscopic formations, like one of those old Busby Berkley numbers only in dazzling color. The dance of color in the dining room merging with the tantalizing aromas from the kitchen was out of this world. No one else in the restaurant appeared to see this symphony of color streaming around and through the people, tables, chairs, and walls. None of it was visible to the mundane eye, even though the color beings filling the restaurant far outnumbered the patrons. Mother H certainly had something good cooking for us here.

I smiled, trying to contain my excitement regarding the mystery of who or what we were about to meet. Sit and Merta seemed to be oblivious to the colors, but I could tell from Din's demeanor that he could see what I was seeing. With a slight nod of his head, he told me to pay attention to whatever happened next.

There were five or six other people waiting in the reception area, but immediately upon greeting us the hostess escorted us to a table in the dining room. We walked right past the others who were waiting, but none of them seemed to notice that we were being seated before them, if they saw us at all.

"You didn't call ahead for reservations, did you, Elise? Sit asked quietly.

I had done nothing of the kind. I just shrugged my shoulders and shook my head.

Our table was a luxurious booth against the western wall. The wall above the booth had been exquisitely painted with a scene from old-time Sicily. The artist had framed the scene with rich green ivy. The picture itself centered on carefully-modeled vines planted in rows that drew the eye into the painting and to the rolling hills in the background. The sparkling waters of the Mediterranean Sea beckoned in the distance far beyond the vineyard.

The land in the painting was alive—really alive—in the way the sunlight permeated through the shading of the yellow-gold, green, and brown. Every vine and grape had been meticulously painted with subtle and differing shades color. I wondered how many hours the artist had spent on this nearly thirty-foot-wide landscape.

The most striking part of the entire masterpiece was the image of a woman standing not quite in the middle of the painting. She had a basket full of olives in one arm, and her black hair was pulled up in a loose bun with a single strand left hanging along her cheek. The warm Sicilian breeze could almost be felt as it caressed her skin. The woman and her smile seemed to be one of contented simplicity.

Perhaps the artist had captured someone's beautiful great-grandmother in the prime of her youth. Whoever the artist was, he or she certainly must have had a strong romantic connection to a particular family's place of origin.

The most alluring details were found in the face and body of the woman herself. The sweat on her brow had a subtle shimmer, but not as glistening as were her dark and timeless eyes. The artist had captured unconditional love and transferred its frequency through the paintbrush into the way the woman gazed outward upon those who looked up at her.

The owners had employed a master artist to adorn their walls with what they probably thought was just another pretty picture for good interior design. What they almost certainly did not know was that the painting oozed aspects of the energy of Mother H. No wonder this restaurant did such good business.

"I wonder who the artist is," Sit said, her tone expressing appreciation of the talent behind the work.

"Where is the artist's signature? I don't see it anywhere," Merta said.

"Are you sure?" Sit turned in her seat and knelt on the booth bench to look more closely at the mural. When Sit was on the trail of a mystery, decorum was the least of her concerns.

Merta joined Sit in the search. Both had their necks craned up at awkward angles, looking as if they were examining a priceless masterpiece hanging on the wall in the Louvre.

"Can you find Waldo?" Din teased.

"Very funny, Mister Book Writer," Merta huffed, looking at him with that stern, matronly Latina look that she gets when Din makes one of his silly jokes.

"I don't think you ladies are going to find anything," Din said. "I believe this artist does not wish to reveal an identity to the world as yet."

Sit and Merta sat. Merta, shrugged her shoulders and Sit continued to gaze intently at the mysterious painting.

"It's so peaceful in here," Sit said. She had finally relaxed and was beginning to absorb more of the surroundings than just the painting.

"Listen to that lovely sound. How beautiful," Merta added dreamily.

"Could this place get any better?" Din questioned.

"You ain't seen nothin' yet," I replied.

The gentle murmur of flowing water emanated from a large fountain in the center of the restaurant, about fifty feet away from where we were seated. It had a delightful array of flora growing in the pool, and, thank God, there were no fish in it. As wonderful as they are, I have never appreciated seeing those monstrous, colorful goldfish in some restaurants' pools. The poor things always look over-crowded and insatiably hungry. The simplicity of the green vines climbing out of the basin of this fountain's pool was sufficient.

I must have been somewhat mesmerized by the sound of the water for I soon found myself speaking my thoughts out loud. "If only there were a perfect fountain such as this in every town, all over the world," I said drowsily. "If more people became transfixed by gazing upon things such as this, then there might be a natural understanding and appreciation of how the Creation Frequency works."

"What exactly do you mean, Elise?" Sit asked.

Her voice brought me back to the moment. I paused to think about what I had just said, then answered, "Well, just observe what the water does in this fountain. Look at the mechanics of it, for starters."

"Ah, yes. It appears to descend from the top, growing in width relative to the basin below it, but keeps rain-ing down until it all collects into one giant pool down beneath." Our Strong Weet scientist, Sit, was studiously analyzing the fountain.

Merta turned her head this way and that in order to see as much of the fountain as possible. She said, "But the magic of the fountain is that you never see the water being re-circulated back up to the top. It just seems like it is a never-ending stream of water gathering itself in the pool below. *Como linda, Diosa!* It is amazing how wondrous and beautiful Our God has made even the simplest of things. I do not think, however, that the water pipes are very pretty to look at. That is why they are hidden somewhere in all those vines, eh?"

My smile grew as I replied, "Right. And that is also why we can't see our own veins and arteries, I suppose. It would be rather ugly if God had made humanity into fleshly organic beings with the vascular system exposed on the outside of the body. Can you imagine?"

"No, I can't. That would be unpleasant to look at," Sit agreed.

I said, "But we were talking about the fountain and the Creation Frequency. We know that the mechanism of the tubing system of the water fountain is always there, right? So long as the electricity fuels the flow of the water, it will keep moving continuously. God is the Source of all energy, but humanity cannot see the plumbing, if you will, that God uses to funnel the energy. Mankind can't see this glorious webbing because Mother took that perceptive ability away from people after millions of years of abusing God. The truth that still makes my jaw drop in wonder is that the waterfall of God's perfect energetic love for everyone, rains down constantly upon all Life even after millennia of horrors done here in this realm."

"What is your take on the fountain, Din?" Sit asked.

"It's got pretty colors and I like it." Din smiled, and everyone laughed.

"Actually, it reminds me of the fountain in the inner courtyard of a hotel I was at in Castellammare del Golfo," Din continued. "I wonder if it's still there after all this time?"

Our conversation was interrupted by the arrival of a young waitress. Her appearance was no-nonsense professional—black pants, a white button-up blouse, black apron at her waist, and her dark brown hair tied back in a tight ponytail—but her manner was warm and welcoming. Her face was unusually pale but beautiful and was graced with a captivating smile.

"Good evening. My name is Christa and I'll be your server. How are you all?"

Din took the lead. "We are all very well, thanks. And you?"

"Sweet. I am sweet, thanks. Would you all care for some drinks before you order? I will give you some time to look over the menu. It's filled with amazing choices, and it might take you awhile, but there is no rush."

Christa took our drink orders and left. She moved with an air of grace as she floated through the numerous other servers who were bustling about the restaurant.

"Seeing all these young people work so hard to wait on others makes me feel a little sad." Merta was watching the bus boy moving with quick efficiency at the table to our left.

"Why would you feel sad about that, Merta? It's a restaurant, it's what they do," Din said.

"Oh, let her have her Hallmark moment, Din." I smiled playfully at Merta, who slapped my hand in her motherly fashion.

Merta continued, "I just do not think that restaurants are a natural thing, made by God, and I feel very confident that there are no restaurants in Heaven. Why would angels want to sweat and wait on other angels, in order to pay for utility bills? It is cruel. Actually, angels do not have utility bills, so I do not even know what I am talking about."

Din, Sit, and I exchanged glances, puzzled at what Merta had apparently pulled out of nowhere to drop into the conversation. By now, however, we were used to the particularities of her sentimental character, so we decided to let it slide as we busied ourselves with the napkins that had been ornately folded and tucked into our water glasses.

"There is something about this restaurant," Sit said. Her face held an expression of deep concentration as she studied the scene in the dining room rather than the pages of her menu. "This place doesn't seem like it fits in down here. I mean, it's a great restaurant, but it just seems too good to be true."

That was when that I sensed a slight movement out of the corner of my eye. I had been holding my menu up so that I could study the endless list of options while maintaining an awareness of the surroundings. I lowered the menu and gave my full attention to discovering the source of the almost imperceptible disturbance. As I scanned the room, my gaze fell upon the figure of the olive bearer in the painting. When we had first seen the lovely figure, she had appeared to be looking at something in the distance far beyond the confines of the restaurant. Now however, her head was angled differently, and her eyes appeared to be focused on the four of us at our table.

I returned my attention to the menu, reserving a small portion of my awareness for the figure in the painting. Such supernatural happenings have become increasingly frequent for all of us and I was curious to see what would happen next. I didn't have long to wait, and this time Merta noticed as well.

"That woman's eyes just blinked three times. Did you all see that? The woman in the painting just winked, *uno, dos, tres*. Please, somebody tell me you saw it too."

"Hmm? What? The painting? I was too busy with the menu to notice," Din said.

"You mean her eyes moved, like in one of those bad horror movies where the old painting of someone's dead great-grandfather starts to come alive?" Sit chuckled playfully. "No, I didn't see it, but maybe she'll do it again."

"She moved alright," I assured her. "And a lot more lies in the purpose of that painting than just good decor, my friends. The artist lives in that painting, and I think she is much closer than we all realize."

The waitress returned with our drinks, laying small square napkins down before carefully placing the tall, curved-at-the-rim glasses in front of each of us. Her bountiful tray also carried a large basket of warm homemade bread, a dish of olive oil and one of balsamic vinegar, and a white ceramic plate mounded with freshly grated Parmesan cheese.

"The bread baskets are bottomless here, so don't hesitate to ask for more," Christa said. "There is always so much more."

"Abundantly more," I said, looking at her intently.

Din shot me a knowing glance and said, "Yes, indeed. Hey, listen Christa, can you tell us anything about that painting on the wall? Do you know who the artist is? We've all been marveling at it. It is phenomenal."

"Thank you. I will let my"—she took in a quick breath—"my manager know you enjoy it. No, I cannot tell you much about the painting. I think it speaks for itself, though. The artist is not around right now, that much I do know."

"Do you know where the artist is from? There is no signature anywhere that we can see," Din said casually as he helped himself to the butter.

Christa smiled. "Yes, it is strange, indeed, but pretty

cool, if you ask me. I am told the artist is not from around here, though."

"Well, Christa, if you are somehow able to get word to the artist please express our deep appreciation for his or her magical nature and gifts if you would." I lifted my glass to take a sip of iced tea.

"I most certainly will. Are you ready to place your order?"

Din and I glanced at each other, aware of Christa's guarded answers.

We ordered, and then proceeded to enjoy the signature homemade bread. We never saw the bottom of the baskets as they were constantly being refilled. Christa seemed to appear from out of nowhere with more bread. The dishes of olive oil, balsamic vinegar, and Parmesan cheese as well were constantly replenished.

It was a perfect dining experience, made ever more-tantalizing by the mystery of the painting and Christa's responses to our questions regarding it and the painter. I felt strongly that the artist was female, and that this unnamed woman was indeed the one we were sent here to meet. But where was she, and how were we to find her?

We passed the time chatting amiably about current newsworthy events, the simple joys of the season, and of the discoveries each of us had been gifted with in the past few months. This Gathering was like a homecoming feast, but there was still someone missing.

Christa reappeared with a gigantic tray loaded with our entrées balanced gracefully and effortlessly on one upraised hand.

Each of us had ordered something different—scrumptious linguine Alfredo, chicken saltimbocca and Parmigiana, and manicotti—but we all agreed to sample the full array of it together. The feasting seemed to go on forever, but after an hour or so our stomachs were calling it quits. We were going to need take-out boxes. I was also in need of the restroom, so I excused myself.

"Be careful where you step," Din said, as I slid out of the booth. "You never know what might appear right in front of your feet."

"Okay, but my dog's at home, and I am not too worried about four-legged critters in this high-class restaurant," I said with a laugh.

The powder room was replete with comfortable chairs, a wall-length mirror, and a table with lotions, tissues, and hand-wipes. It was dimly lit, and luxurious. I was sure our bill would reflect the luxury, but truly fulfilling experiences like these are worth it.

I walked in to find Christa standing in front of the mirror. She turned quickly and bent down to retrieve the pencil and pocket-size sketch pad that lay within inches of my feet near the powder room door where she had apparently dropped them. She stuffed them back into her apron pocket and stood up, her eyes directly meeting my gaze.

"So, what's your name?" she blurted out with an air of discomfort.

"I am called Elise. The way you pronounce your name, *Crees-ta*, is exactly the way I would have pronounced it, had I given my daughter such a beautiful name."

"Where do you come from? You and your friends are not from around here." Christa seemed a little uneasy, perhaps surprised by her own blunt and unabashed directness. There was an odd assortment of energy bouncing about the room.

"We come from very far away. I don't live in this town anymore, but I was born here. We came back to St. Louis for a little field trip of sorts, and we were drawn here for our meal. What about you? Where do you come from?"

Christa's eyes were focused directly on my own as she slowly inhaled and seemed to consider carefully what she would say next.

"Ditto, except for the part about the field trip and being drawn to come here. I draw where I want to go, and then go there."

I was confused by her statement. Christa had answered in a perplexing, almost riddle-like fashion that did not make much sense at first.

"So, you come from very far away and you don't live in this town but you were born here? Wow, you must spend a lot on gas for your car," I said, smiling.

Then we both smiled, for the strangeness of our conversation warranted it. Christa seemed to relax a bit, but there were still a lot of unanswered questions.

I got the impression that Christa wasn't one who opened up easily with most people. Our interaction was unique and weird, just like her answers to us at the dinner table regarding the artist of the mural.

Christa composed herself, found another piece of paper in her apron pocket and scribbled something as she spoke. "Listen, I have to get back to my tables, but I have to talk with you more." She finished writing and held out the paper. "Here's my number, Eeee—"

"—lise. Elise." I reached out my right hand to receive the paper from her left.

"Right. Elise."

"Absolutely, Christa. You'll hear from me very soon. And thank you for reaching out."

She smiled as she floated through the restroom door, but not before turning to look at me one last time.

"Oh, and Christa," The words came out of me as if they had their own mind. "I would love to see your other masterpieces sometime. If ever you might be ready to share more of your amazing paintings, I'd be all eye."

Christa seemed stunned for just a second before saying, "You mean you'd be 'all eyes,' right?"

I shook my head, "No, I meant it exactly the way I said it. You are the artist of that splendid mural out there, yes?"

Christa paused for a long moment. She looked down at her feet and then replied hesitantly, "Yes, I am. But please, do not speak a word of it to anyone, okay? This is very, very important. No one must know."

My heart swelled and my eyes began to water as I saw the comforting light of a female spirit being surrounding Christa. This sweet being knew, loved, and cherished Christa and was also asking me to abide by her request.

"I honor your wishes. My lips are sealed, and I shall speak of it to no one. You have my word."

I walked back to the table where Din, Merta, and Sit were looking both impatient and curious.

"What happened? Did you get sucked in? Or did you stumble on something in there? I told you to watch your step, didn't I?" Din asked playfully, and of course, I knew that he knew all that had transpired.

"No, I just got distracted by the pretty colors, that's all."

Din left money in the black check billfold. "Take care of your part of this right away. I don't want that kind of cash sitting around for the busboy, y'hear?" he told Christa as he handed it to her.

She smiled. "Thank you. I will take my part immediately."

How prophetic were her words.

***

Painting the Body into Being:
The Mastery of Christa

Christa is a tough, silent young woman whose spirit is driven by her painting. She is sweet and pure. When I watch her gazing at something with her dark Italian doe-like eyes, I can almost feel her painting the object or person with tender attention. She walks and breathes her passion for brush and color, and, with great focus, she is bringing something uniquely magical into this plane of existence

Only three days had passed since our exchange in the powder room in St. Louis, when she contacted me by telephone, but it was many weeks before she really began to open up, sharing tidbits of her secret universe of mastery. The Strong Weet came to know her more by way of observing the paintings she was willing to show us rather than through our conversations with her.

Between her job at the Italian restaurant and her painting, Christa had very little in the way of free time, so we were pleased to accept her invitation to drive to St. Louis for the sole purpose of viewing some of her work. Merta was not able to go with us, as she had some church obligations she had to attend to. She made us promise to apologize to Christa for not being there and to give a detailed description of Christa's art on our return.

"Please understand that I will only be showing you just a few of my paintings," was the only message she left on my voice mail after I had called to confirm that we were on our way to St. Louis.

On the drive in, Sit commented, "Christa sure is a strange one. I wonder why she is so secretive about her work? I'm sure she has good reason, but so many people would benefit tremendously from simply laying eyes on her creations. I don't think I have ever seen paintings that exude such life as I see in hers."

Din was driving but replied, "Christa is a Strong Weet, and she walks with her own kind of knowing about it. I think it is impressive that she chooses to be silent about her work. I am not sure what she is aware of regarding where she comes from, but it is wonderful that she is a spirit being who is truly living her path with such drive. Elise, what has she told you about herself? You're the only one she's talked to."

"All I know is what you all have observed as well. She has good reason to be a quiet master, and it will be a gift if we learn more of how she's contributing to The Great Plan. I only hope that she will come to trust us enough to tell us more about herself. I am excited to see the paintings she's willing to show us, that's for sure."

"Christa is certainly a loner, but I get no sense of her being lonely," Sit said.

"A rebel with a cause," Din added.

"And lots of paintbrushes," I added.

After the hour and a half drive into St. Louis, we finally arrived at Christa's apartment building. We walked up to the second floor, found her door, and knocked. She opened it immediately.

"Hi there. Come on in. I've got everything all set up." Christa smiled at us warmly.

We entered her spacious studio apartment, which was bright with the light from the floor-to-ceiling windows along the south-facing wall.

"Golly, you hardly need artificial light with a place like this. It's so bright in here," Sit observed.

"Yes, well, I actually don't use a whole lot of it as it is. I'm up early and I go to bed early, usually." Christa wiped her hands on her paint stained jeans. "I'm sorry that I don't have any snacks, but I do have tea, if you'd like some."

"Well, actually, we're still digesting the meal we had the other day at the restaurant where you work, so we're doing just fine, thanks." We all chuckled at Din's joke.

"That was over a month ago," Christa said. "You guys must be aliens or something. Or maybe you just have really slow metabolisms."

"There is, indeed, nourishment beyond food." I gave Christa a knowing look. "As the artist you are, you seem to thrive off your paintings alone."

"Follow me." Christa motioned us toward a section of her studio where she'd arranged five of her paintings for viewing. They were uniform in size, about four feet long by three-and-a-half feet tall, and She had set them up on easels that were evenly spaced in a semi-circle and positioned comfortable chairs to face them at the best distance for viewing. Sit, Din, and I sat while Christa remained standing.

The images were all of human bodies in various settings and degrees of reality. I was particularly drawn to the painting of a woman's form that appeared also to be some kind of space nebula. It was a trick on the eyes. When it was observed from one angle, the woman's body was clearly visible, but when the angle of view was changed the form disappeared, merging into a collection of stars and streams of color. The intricately painted shading and hues of the woman's face, neck and shoulders were transformed into a stream of intergalactic star dust with a turn of one's own head.

Din moved closer to examine a painting of a young girl standing on the surface of the water in the middle of an ocean. "This work is truly awesome, Christa."

The third painting was a full-face portrait of a man

looking out of the canvas and straight into the heart of the observer. The deep furrows of his brow spoke of years of hardship, and his eyes were those of a soul that longed to be free from the story of his life. From a distance, the man's image called out for the observer to come closer. Upon approach, one almost wanted to turn away. It was as if the suffering of this person was written in the detailed scars of his cheeks, weathered skin, and pallid color.

The fourth painting was of two lovers intertwined in an embrace, their combined figures merging into a sort of tree of light. The glistening moisture on their skin was enough to raise anyone's body temperature and quicken the breath, but it was the sunshine exploding behind their forms that made the whole of the painting such a titillating feast to the spirit mind.

The fifth painting was covered with a purple cloth so that it could not be seen.

We studied her work in silence for about thirty minutes, then I asked, "Do we get to see that one, Christa?"

She smiled enigmatically and replied, "Only if you are ready."

Din and I looked at each other, knowing that something huge was about to be revealed. Sit stared with great focus at the covered art.

"Ready." Sit smiled.

Christa stood in front of the painting and, using both hands, gently raised the purple veil. She draped the cloth over the back of the painting and stepped aside.

"Whoa," Din said as he took a step back.

It was a portrait of Mother H, and it was rendered as realistically and accurately as humanly possible. Her eyes pierced through the fibers of the canvas into every cell of our bodies. Her skin glowed against the backdrop of a pitch-black sky, and her raised arms seemed about to bring forth the final end to all of life. Christa had managed to do something unique and superb—or rather, something uniquely superb had come through Christa into this image of Mother.

While the painting certainly portrayed Mother as the Great Being of Destruction, which she is, it was imbued with a living energy of sincere tenderness that emanated from the whole of her Body. It had nothing to do with the colors or the form or the shading or the hue of the image of Mother—Mother was present in this painting. The fullness of Mother radiated from the painted surface, and we were all speechless.

It was clear to us now why Christa had remained quiet about being the one responsible for such powerful paintings. The pure force of Mother and God radiated through each painting, and the paintings needed to speak for themselves. She told us later that she felt that by claiming personal identity for their creation she would detract from their energetic gift. The great humility in her choice to remain anonymous made her artistic mastery all the more amazing.

We basked in the Glow of Christa's works for fully an hour. We didn't speak as we switched places to change our viewpoint, sometimes sitting, sometimes standing. Christa stood the entire time, with her arms folded, watching us view her works.

We had arrived in mid-afternoon, and it was now getting dark outside. Our ability to study the paintings was waning due to the fading light, but before we were able to speak of leaving, Christa went to a cupboard and brought out three candles. She lit them and carried them carefully back to where they could illuminate the paintings.

No one spoke. No one wanted to speak. We sat for another half hour enjoying the absolute quiet and stillness in the candlelight.

Din was the first to get up to put his coat on, with Sit and me reluctantly following suit. Still, there was not a sound uttered. We made our way to the door, each of us pausing to wordlessly share our thoughts with Christa. When it was my turn to leave, I reached out for her hands. She accepted, and for just a moment I held hers, gentle and perfect, cupped in my own. We stood silently together for several heartbeats, then each of us smiled at the other and I followed Din and Sit out to the car.

ANNIE INTRODUCES THE ONE BODY

You have been told repeatedly that if humanity does not return to God and correct the disconnected thinking, all life on Earth will end. That is the message that you need to understand. What Elise and Father will continue to teach, is that God is totally focused on you, your happiness, and your well-being. He is a personal God and has a specific frequency of attention tuned to you, holding true to the vision of all that you may become. All aspects of your growth and all the details of your life are of deep concern to God.

God also wants you to get with the cosmic program, so to speak, and live as a spirit being so that you may help the whole of humanity to have a secure future. It must start, however, with your personal determination to find solace, contentment, and healing in God. In all truth, there is no distinction between your personal fulfillment in God and the future of humanity. Indeed, life is one in that respect.

Everything you need is right here for you now — in front of you, above, below, this way, that way, and most especially, within you. This everything is the Body of God, and this instructional volume you hold in your hands is a vibration, the materialization of a unique message written for and of God's Body, of which you are a part. Although you are not God, your life — your body, your mind, your spirit — is already a part of this one Body of His Creation. This book, especially the following sections, will be here for you to interfuse with this everlasting reality and truth.

I like Elise's word, interfuse, because she is exactly right in how she uses it. The human mind must be interfused — poured together — with the spirit mind, meaning that the conscious mind must be permeated with the higher ways of thinking, relating to that which is far above and beyond the things of this world. This is the goal that should consume the mind of every individual who is serious about seeing a future in which humanity is living within the Creation of God. If it is too hard to focus on the future well-being of all people on Earth, simply realize that we want you to experience and know the awesome powers of complete happiness and health, and the boundlessness contained within your DNA. That is what happens when you choose to live as a child of God. It is your birthright to be fulfilled in this life.

You will learn more about this One Body of God later, but for now, be patient and willing to learn how to remember.

The best remedy for now is to go out and spend as much time as possible in nature. This will bring comfort to any doubting mind, for there is no questioning of what nature is. There is no dictating to the skies of what they will bring, day by day, so there must be a natural acceptance of its wondrous mystery. Simply by placing yourself more frequently within nature and by studying these volumes of Mary's Diary, your mind will absorb the truth, and the attributes of God will slowly be revealed to you and through you.

The whole of life is depending on you to live by this. Humanity has issues of control and domination only because mankind has chosen to abuse itself by becoming victim to personal power and ego in grotesque forms. Belonging to God is entirely different. It is complete and perfect freedom because you are awakened to the truth that all of God's promises are real. You become experienced in the Creations of God as you go about your life in devotional worship.

When it becomes firmly fixed in your mind that the whole of yourself belongs to God, you will begin to discover the joy in this. You are truly free when you live in this way, and you will be a slave to nothing and no one.

Din Reflects on Nature

Not so very long ago, before Mary started popping in and out of my head, I used to come out here to the garden simply to find a place of peace and quiet after a hard day's work. I would sit here under this blessed Linden tree for as long as I possibly could, taking in the tranquility I felt within the presence of such a glorious creation. Of course, back then I didn't have the knowledge or the experiences I have today, so all I was really feeling within myself was a superficial awareness that there must be some sort of energetic difference between myself and the things of nature. I had no idea of the journey I was about to begin later that night, when I heard those five words spoken softly to my mind while getting ready for bed:

I would speak with you.

The afternoon before the evening that would change my life forever, I was sitting in this exact same spot, with my eyes closed, and my mental gymnastics on hold while I took pleasure in the sound of the birds chirping, the touch of the breeze on my skin, and the smell of the flowers all around. Oh, to be sure, this garden was a beautiful spot to behold even then. It was a peaceful place, regardless of the time of day or night; a refuge from the rest of my somewhat chaotic little world. It even had a magical quality about it that I would often ponder in an attempt to explain to myself within the limitations of what I knew before Mary opened up the universe before me.

This sweet little place was just a garden to me—a mere backyard to most people. But suddenly, after my awakening and my immersion into the dimensions that lie beyond those in plain sight, the backyard became a paradise.

A garden of daisies became a Garden of Eden. This little plot of earth revealed its true identity. The frequencies of all the energies of the ages released themselves in one single moment of incredible drama and unbelievable splendor. Annica arose.

My life has not been the same since. If I could play the role of Mary for a moment and implant one pivotal thought in the minds of everyone on this world, I would seed within them this single image, an image that is more than a mere mental picture, it is a promise from God: There is not a square inch of soil on this planet that is not connected to Annica. Everyone's backyard can become a Garden of Eden, for the Garden of Eden is not located somewhere in Mesopotamia or Africa or wherever, it is the entire Planet Earth. Every single backyard everywhere on this world is resonating with frequencies that are connected directly with Annica. All anyone needs to do is develop a true sense of harmony with the life force of where they are.

Din Introduces the Concept of Hozhoni

I've been asked by Annie to discuss a subject that is extremely important to this world, yet it gets very little attention. I'm going to write about harmony. In a way, this will be sort of a "State of the Planet" report. Actually, more of a "State of the Relationship of Humanity to Nature" report, filled with true hope and promise.

From the word *harmony* you get *harmonize*, which occurs when two or more elements of different essences combine together and bring about the perfection of the whole. A great example of this would be four singers: a high tenor, a bass, a baritone, and a low tenor. All are different talents, all can be good when performing by themselves, but when you bring them together as a barbershop quartet, the result can be perfect harmony.

Harmony and perfection are closely related. The Navajo have a word, *hozhoni*, which means both perfection and/or harmony. Similarly, the Hebrew word, *lev*, illustrates the two different concepts of the physical heart and the thoughts of the mind. In fact, like the quartet, *hozhoni* has four separate elements: balance, perfection, beauty, and peace. The Navajo give these four elements practical life applications as well. Balance is represented by self-control, perfection by love, beauty by wholeness, and peace by higher awareness. In Navajo beliefs, when all four of these elements act together as one, the result is pure harmony. If you are living in pure Navajo *hozhoni*, then these four elements are all present in your life and working together. If any one of these elements is missing, your life is out of balance with all nature around you, and you are in a state of disharmony.

Unfortunately, this is the state many people living in the semi-chaos of our rather freewheeling society find themselves in, reflecting the disharmony between the way they perceive "who they are", and their surroundings. If you don't have peace in your heart, or if you can't see the beauty of your own nature, that will indeed cause disharmony within you, and the result will manifest in illness, emotional instability, depression, bad attitudes, and other problems that plague the minds of people all over this world. Just as important, if you don't have peace in your surroundings, it will also cause disharmony in your life capable of producing trouble with your neighbors, your family, your friends, and even nature itself.

Nature, too, has four elements that, when combined—like the barbershop quartet—can create beauty, peace, and harmony in nature. If any one of these is off, the result is disharmony. Unfortunately, that is where you find yourselves today. Nature is a bit out of balance, and it isn't getting any better. You have air and water pollution, droughts and floods, earthquakes, fires, tornadoes, tsunamis, hurricanes—the list goes on, and there is very little that mankind alone can do to stop any of these natural disruptions. The power of nature is far greater than any quick fix humanity can lay upon it. It requires great effort, much determination, and, perhaps, even a helping hand from somewhere else in order to repair the damage that has been done.

Fifty years ago, you never heard of things such as greenhouse effect, climate change, global warming, or hole in the ozone layer, but now they are common phrases used in almost every home. Granted, much of the hype is total nonsense. For this world, as for all worlds in this universe, growth and decay, weather changes, and a number of other factors are natural, on-going cycles having nothing to do with humans or human activity. When seen from the human perspective, the results of this cyclic activity are disastrous and becoming increasingly so as the Earth's population increases. That doesn't mean that improvements in your behaviors will do nothing to protect Earth. Quite the opposite, in fact. Because of your dependence on nature for your survival, you need to do everything you can to help Mother Nature—Mother H—in as many ways as you can.

The sad thing is that you seem to be totally unaware of the fact that the real threat to the Creation Frequency is not global warming but the evil thoughts of seven billion people accumulating and spreading an evil frequency out into the atmosphere, where it attacks the Creation Frequency with a vengeance. That is not the fault of nature. Humanity is responsible, so it is up to humanity to alter the global communal lifestyle that produces such a constant stream of depraved thoughts, so that the damage that has been done to the Creation Frequency can be healed.

Let's bring this all back down to a personal level. It's the general order of things that nature has a built-in balancing process of its own; a corrective mechanism that allows healing and purification when things go wrong.

When pollutants are no longer dumped into clear streams, eventually the pollutants will be filtered out and the water returned to a purified state. When smog is not being pumped into the air by automobiles and the like, the air will eventually be cleansed. When tree bark is cut or marred in some way, if allowed to heal on its own, the bark will eventually repair itself by scabbing over, much like human skin, repairing the damage in a relatively short period of time. But the Creation Frequency is not immune to such a pounding as it receives daily upon this world. It cannot repair itself without help.

What must also be considered, is that if the damage is overwhelming, the natural healing process cannot keep up with it, and that is the problem confronting humanity today. The damage being done is so overwhelming that nature cannot defend or repair itself effectively.

What does all this nature talk have to do with humans on the personal level? It has everything to do with humans. It isn't just that mankind uses and misuses nature, but that human beings are nature. Yes, human spirits are eternal, and are made from an energy source they may never fully understand until they cross over, but their physical bodies are pure nature. The same elements that give life to trees, mountain streams, clouds, yellow daisies, wild deer, desert sand, and boulders, are the same elements that animate human bodies: earth, air, fire, and water. All of those things of nature are like cousins here in this plane of existence. In reality, they are really not much different from people; their physical elements are the same. The major difference between hemoglobin found in human blood and chlorophyll found in green plants is that chlorophyll contains magnesium, and hemoglobin contains iron. Hemoglobin is essential to humans — and all red-blooded creatures — to carry oxygen to the cells of the body. Chlorophyll is the substance in green plants that allows them to convert the energy of sunlight to a form that can be stored and used for growth and activity. Both of these molecules are composed of the same four basic elements — carbon, hydrogen, oxygen, and nitrogen — arranged in an elegant pattern somewhat like a snowflake, and at the center of the snowflake is a single atom of a metal — iron for hemoglobin, magnesium for chlorophyll. Plants convert and store the energy of the sun, releasing oxygen in the process. You consume the energy stored in plants and breathe in the oxygen, releasing carbon dioxide, which in turn is used by plants in the process of converting sunlight to food.

It would be a wonderful thing if everyone on Earth were to become aware of these facts and take them to heart. It would change the way humanity looks at everything. If everyone knew that the tree growing out in their own back yard was their cousin, it just might change the way mankind confronts certain issues. Native Americans teach in their old ways that all the nature beings are related to the humans. Everything is family. Trees and rocks and animals and clouds are called their brothers and sisters and cousins. I believe people would think twice before harming one of nature's own, if they believed they were harming a sentient being that might even be related to them.

Human beings really are something special. Nearly every religion on this planet has a scripture defining the human body as the house, dwelling, or temple of the Spirit of God, a temple in which God allows a small part of the very Spirit that created the universe to reside, as long as the Spirit is welcome there. The human body is a sacred vessel that houses the Spirit of eternal creation. But many humans, if not most, do not treat their vessels any differently than they treat their forests. Just as humans have a tendency to pollute nature, they also pollute their bodies with chemicals and additives that have no business being in the human system.

The human body is meant to be a cathedral, not unlike the beautiful cathedrals found throughout the world. How many would go into St. Peter's Cathedral and spray paint graffiti on the walls? In effect, that is what a person does every time they add something to their body that isn't harmonious to their physical nature.

If all things—including temples, bodies, and cathedrals—are made of the same elemental earth, air, fire, and water, then what does that make the entire Earth? The most beautiful and the most wondrous cathedral ever built. Those who have visited natural parks or camped in the wilderness know exactly what I am writing about. The Earth is God's cathedral for this part of the galaxy. It is to be respected and protected.

Humans have been given many wonderful natural resources to use, such as timber for their houses, oil for their cars, and water for energy and for their crops, but these are gifts to be used with respect and gratitude. It seems though, that modern humanity has laid aside the role of steward and conservator for that of user and consumer, and in that role has gone way beyond moderation. Like everything else humans do, they do it to the extreme. They over use. They abuse their own life resources, not just here in the US, but all around the world. In fact, the US is one of the most environmentally aware and protective countries on Earth. But everyone everywhere, regardless of political affiliation, race, gender, or religion, shares the blame for the situation they find themselves in today. There is a solution, but it isn't found in casting stones at each other, or in fuming with rage as a part of an organized demonstration. It is found in love and in blessing the Earth and blessing each other with the love that God has placed inside each and every human.

How many people think of themselves as being a saint? A person doesn't have to be formally canonized by the Pope to be a saint. Even the Pope himself has said that most of the true saints have never been canonized. They have never been recognized by a church or religion at all. They are so highly evolved as spiritual beings that they aren't even noticed by the world around them. Mother Teresa was a perfect example of this until the media discovered her. There are thousands of other saints that have not yet been discovered. They simply live their lives with respect for nature and gratitude for the gifts God has given to them.

What exactly is it that turns a person into a saint? Miracles! One of the qualifications for being recognized as a saint by the church is that a person must have at least two proven miracles attributed to their influence after their death.

Miracles have to do with the manipulation of the elements of nature in a seemingly unnatural way, and every canonized saint was recognized for his or her ability to do this. This is found not just in the Catholic Church. Nearly every religion on Earth has this same requirement for an equivalent designation. Every potential saint must also have a close association with nature itself. Most have actually lived out in nature in caves, huts, and deserts. Many wrote volumes of work on how nature had influenced them in everything they did while they were alive, especially in their actual trials and tribulations on the journey to become the saint that they are now recognized to be. They were in harmony with nature. They were Hozhoni.

Saint Teresa of Avila wrote several books during her lifetime. In them, she compared the spiritual life of a saint to the life of a gardener. She produced dozens of beautiful, simple metaphors for the gentle act of gardening, and how working in a garden resembles the daily life of a spiritual person.

Saint Therese of Lisieux is frequently referred to as the Little Flower of Jesus, because that is the image she used in describing herself. She meant it as a metaphor for others to adopt in their own lives—a sweet picture of a pretty little flower, opening its dainty petals to God every morning, and then closing them in the evening, to fall asleep in the trust and protection of God.

Saint John of the Cross compared his life to being in utter darkness without a guide, in the midst of a storm with lightning and thunder and all the dramatic insults nature could hurl upon him. He called this his "Dark Night of the Soul." It was a frightening thing for any person to go through, but when he came out the other side, he found himself inside the Light of God. It brought him onto the path of sainthood.

Saint Francis of Assisi preached to birds and the wolves. He called the sun his brother and the moon his sister. The trees and the plants were all his cousins, and he treated them with great respect, conversing with them daily, caring for them, praying for their safety as if they really were his closest relatives.

Sainthood has very little to do with church or religion, and you certainly don't attain your sainthood by walking around looking pious all day or by doing dozens of little spiritual exercises in an attempt to please God. You get there by recognizing your own true relation to nature, and by walking in harmony with nature. You get there by walking the floor of this "Great Cathedral Earth" as one who is mindful of the sacredness of everything around you. You get there by realizing that you are not the shallow accumulation of things society wants you to be. There is a section in *The Strong Witch Society* in which I described how all of nature exploded around me in the Annican Garden. That was my first initiation into a state of mind of total hozhoni. Yes, Mary was working her magic within me in order for me to be able to "see" what it was that I was seeing. But after that wonderful experience, that great gift from God has not left me. The same gift can be yours regardless of who you are, if you only open yourself to the true reality God is willing to share with you. You must first cast aside any preconceived notions you have acquired from society about how nature's Spirit is supposed to appear to mankind, for what is projected on the surface is far from the magnificent essence found at the heart of God's Great Creation.

The images we have of saints from all religions are heart-warming and good, but they are not limited to a handful of canonized humans who have been discovered by the populace and then placed on pedestals for all to adore. The discovery can also be made inside you, and anyone else, simply by recognizing your true identity as a spirit being of wonderful essence, intricately interwoven with every facet and fiber of the entirety of Creation; a beautiful being who was originally meant to walk in harmony with all of nature, simply because you *are* nature, and you *are* harmony. Just because humanity has become disoriented and removed from the original intent of the Founders of this world, does not mean that those alive today cannot reclaim their destiny. It only takes a few strong, personal frequencies to fulfill that promise — self-control, and a determined human will desirous of living within the Will of God.

Many people have asked me over the years, "What is my purpose in life?" My answer is that the purpose is the same for everyone: Not to live for human will, but to live in the Will of God. That is what will bring perfect hozhoni to this world, for the Will of God is the very essence of pure harmony.

ELISE SPEAKS OF ABSOLUTE HEALING

Obsession with physical perfection and the pursuit of healing without commitment are rampant in the western world. In addition, the merchandising of ideas falsely labeled as spirituality is raking in millions of dollars from a growing horde of ever-hungry seekers.

The list of products, experts, TV shows, magazines, blogs, forums, seminars, and books marketed to starving consumers looking for all the answers to their physical, mental, and spiritual problems is endless. In a world that produces such an abundance of experts who are offering—for a price—secrets to cure all ailments to a populace willing to support the industry, why are millions still hungry, overweight, depressed, and dying of diseases? These are the circumstances of this three-dimensional reality and antithesis of God's Agenda of perfect life for all.

We must look at the contradictions of the reality. Hundreds of millions of people are overweight and suffering the consequences of that condition, while at least as many, if not more, go without adequate food and water.

Billions, perhaps trillions, of dollars are spent on psychiatric drugs, administered around the world, the demand for them being fueled and funded by pharmaceutical companies and backed up by the *Diagnostic and Statistical Manual of Mental Disorders*. This massive tome compiled by a committee of psychiatrists is widely used to define, classify, and label problematic variations of human behavior, identifying the symptoms and designating them as medical conditions. Sign the sickness into being and the money flows. Hundreds of millions of people on this planet believe what they are told, and thus the imprisonment of the human mind is propagated and enforced.

The reality is that people make choices directed by negative thinking, which leads to increasingly disjointed behaviors and causes people to become unhealthy and out of sync with physical reality on Earth. Continued negative thinking allows the symptoms of disease to increase in number and severity and to become imprinted into human physiology thus providing the profiteers with further opportunities to label and assign a drug to "remedy" the condition.

Spiritual disconnection feeds a diseased and disconnected body of mankind, leading to negative thoughts that contrive to bear false information which then results in bodies and minds behaving in accordance to such thoughts. Minds and bodies behaving negatively will feed more fatalistic thoughts and dangerously false information to the individual and to the masses.

There is a spiritual void in the collective body and mind of humankind. Humankind has embarked on a superficial quest only to find limited answers to questions of physical, mental, and spiritual health. These so-called answers are greedily consumed by a physically and spiritually starving audience and passed along to become codified on the popular talk shows by a charismatic "guru," and endorsed as truth by repetition on Facebook, Twitter, or Instagram. Thus a diet, product, or healing modality becomes humanity's latest and greatest answer to perfect health or wholeness.

But the cycle works in reverse, as well. In reality, the only way to true health and wholeness is to live your life loving God. Only in that way will one find all answers and solutions to health issues of any kind.

God's plan includes perfect spiritual health for all, and Mother H has done everything in her power for millennia to make sure that everything is arranged on this planet so that humanity may experience this. The patterned network of the physical body, which is actually a spirit body, is an essential component of this perfection.

One result of the mental disconnection from God is that people have lost the ability to listen to their own bodies and are no longer able to recognize the inherent relationship of themselves to the Earth, to the cosmos, and to unconditional love. In spite of the abundance of scientific knowledge regarding the identity of the human body with the elements of the Earth, there is no collective understanding of the identity of human life to nature or the stars. The cells of the body, in particular those of the blood, are refreshed and renewed as a result of the constant death and rebirth of the cells of the flesh. Knowing that the blood is the carrier of ever-streaming life, it would seem that the collective species would be naturally drawn to an appreciation for the wonders of life of which it is a small part, yet there is no true and complete *hozhoni* currently in humanity's collective thinking.

There is no collective desire to return to the experience of physical and spiritual purity. The vices of this world, insidious, abundant, and available to all, maintain a stranglehold on the spirit body of mankind.

In order to return to the vision of a whole and loving humanity as presented by the Strong Weet, it is important to ponder the nature of a collective consciousness living in Godly health. If we were to exist in such a state of *hozhoni*, then we would experience a global culture of well-being in which all peoples understand that the sacred perfection of the essence of Earth is the same as that of the body. People would then strive to live with respect and honor for God Who brings forth life. True worship of God in daily life would consist of the giving of thanks for the spirit beings of food, learning how food is grown and cared for, the study of its origins and of the traditions honoring the gift. What a wonderful world this could be.

The physiology of mankind would begin to change, becoming physically sound and inherently connected to and aware of the rest of the cosmos. The DNA of the flesh would once again be in harmony with the vibration of the Creation Frequency, allowing full expression and use of all the hidden *clairs*: clairvoyance, clairaudience, clairsentience, and claircognizance. That would indeed be the beginning of infinity, for with collective sight that is cosmic and is of God's Will, the limits of communication, travel, and life itself are removed, and a pervasive mentality of awe and wonder would exist. The mystery of life and reverence would be the impetus for the quest for knowledge of health and wholeness. After a period of time, if humanity is indeed granted more time, the life on Earth would exist in a state of *hozhoni*.

The disconnection of humanity from the spirit of wholeness, which is health, is the third most serious problem facing mankind, personal power and ego being the first two, but the choice to ignore or reject the commonality of human life to all life could have far greater consequences. Each individual who wakes up, rejects the ideation of the world and of the past, and embraces the eternal truth that God alone is love and life brings this disconnection one step closer to repair.

ELISE IS INSTRUCTED BY MOTHER H

Daughter, you must speak to the reader directly. Stop speaking to them as if you are standing behind a lectern. I give you permission to make your communication as personal as you wish in order for it to be effective. The humans must understand truth about the body.

Teach them Truth regarding who owns the One Body of which they are a part. Give them imagery to see The Body in their own way. Teach them how to live in this way again. Remind them of how it became such that they think of their lives as belonging to themselves. They are destroying their own place within life, and they need to know exactly what to do and how to correct this.

Mother, I will do my best, and I thank you. I know you are here to speak through me. How do I portray The Body of The All, when so many are imprisoned in the addiction to the physical world? How can I even attempt to? People do not need any special or secret techniques to attain spirit—they just need to break away from the lies that have been sold to them.

The God Who Heals and the Great Tree of Life

The Hebrew name, *Jehovah Rapha*, is derived from a vibration of Hectaran origin and means the *Lord Who Heals*. We speak of the radiance of Jehovah Rapha with awe and appreciation, and we pray that millions upon this planet will choose to receive Its eternal Presence.

God made a gift of the image of the Great Tree of Life to specific groups of people scattered across this planet. Although the sacred knowledge of how Jehovah Rapha spreads the supernatural energy of healing through the Tree was lost, the image of the Tree has become a common theme among many cultures around the world.

In this section of the diary, we will be referring to Jehovah Rapha, and to the image of the Great Tree of Life so that we may create an accurate picture of the energetic presence of God as the exclusive Healer. The knowledge presented in this section of the book provides the keys to life, vitality, and healing for this planet, and it will be of great benefit to you and to all of humanity.

Your body consists of a skeletal framework that supports and protects the fleshly organs. We explained in *The Lost Revelation* that those organs are actually nations of star-matter in their sub-atomic essence. The form that we now recognize as the human body is one that has been reduced to a fleshly mass of organic compounds. It took millions of years for the transformation to produce what has become our physical reality. During that time the energy and light that formed the vessels that contained our spirit-beings was rejected and changed by the accumulation of destructive thoughts. This darkness of thought also caused the consciousness of humans to disconnect from the Will of God, thereby allowing each individual to believe—wrongly—that each life is something that belongs to the self, and is to be governed as each individual desires.

The condition of the physical flesh remains, along with God's love, within the mind of Mother H, and within the core of the Great Tree.

You are connected to the Great Tree of Life through your own branches and roots—your bones, nerves, capillaries, veins, and arteries—and there is no escaping Jehovah Rapha's healing. In order to receive this in full, you must first love God with purity and in all you do.

There is more to human physiology than just the simple channels of transport for electricity, oxygen, and blood that carry the physical life force throughout your body. The network of life that animates your body is a wonderful circuit of cosmic energy connected directly to the grid of the Creation Frequency. It is this grid that links all living bodies to the Great Tree, whose sole purpose is to keep you knowing that you belong to God in the vibrating hum of life. The Great Tree allows you to feel the inter-universal cross-current of life feeding you the nourishing energies of joy, peace, bliss.

What we are revealing to you here is an eternal truth that is encoded into the very DNA that directs your body's growth, form, and function. The information relayed here is intended to trigger your memories and to activate the star-nations comprising your flesh, so that they will be brought into harmony with the Will of God. As long as you do not pollute your body and mind with negative frequencies, and as long as you are determined to live God's Will, you will receive this directly and in great strength and it will be of benefit to you.

The Great Tree of Life, breathing and reaching,

creating and replenishing its sacred fruits, spans across all universes, knows no boundaries, and is controlled exclusively by God. Its vibrating branches support every sub-atomic particle and wave of life, wherever life is found. Its enormity is incomprehensible to the conscious human mind, but as every being is a part of it, we call it forth now as an image that will enhance understanding.

The Tree is actually one enormous body of light, resonating with cosmic and supernatural sound. It streams forth light, mostly White, Blue, and Silver, with variations of hue to meet specific needs in any given space of any universe. There is much darkness emanating from Earth today. Earth can do only so much to counteract the poisons and will soon reach its limit. The Great Tree is pouring forth new healing energies to neutralize the negativity and assist in the maintenance life. The wash of light is a cosmic filtration system that cleanses, restores, and rejuvenates all beings that have the need.

As the dark, jagged negativity is expelled from Earth, it is filtered through the net of the Golden web of the Creation Frequency. It is released into the heart of the Great Tree where it is completely transformed into a purified frequency suitable for the sustenance of life on this planet and elsewhere.

The beating of your heart, the way the cells of your bone marrow swim in a vibratory hum, the fire nation dancing in the electrical pathways of your brain, the sound of your blood whooshing through your arteries—these are all a part of the working of the body of the Great Tree. The dying and rebirthing of the whole of your body's cells are the ebb and flow of the breath of Spirit through the Tree, portioned out to you for your specific needs.

While all this exorcism and cleansing is going on for the whole of the Earth and its inhabitants, each individual is graced with the beauteous rebirthing energy of life. All beings are given that kind of love by God

Whatever is of life is also of the Great Tree. It throbs and pulses living radiance continuously through you and all beings, regardless of whether a being has taken on a physical form or not, for all spirit beings, in or out of body, need Its nourishment. The Great Tree is the transmitter of all life frequencies but is not the originator of them. That is a privilege held only by God.

The cosmic vibration of the Great Tree makes all speech unnecessary, yet The Tree makes use of the breath of creatures in the three-dimensional realm to make itself known. When you focus prayerfully on the breath, you become empowered. The force of the Tree consumes the mind and body, combining them and nurturing them in unity, and peace.

The Great Tree of Life also plays a central part in the transmission of spirit beings into temporal vessels. After being assigned by God and agreeing in contract to take on a specific form, all spirit beings of Earth pass through the Great Tree before arriving at their destination in a temporal form. After being transformed from light energy into a kind of supernatural seed, the spirit being travels up the intricate passageways of the roots and trunk, emerges as a finished "cosmic fruit", then "falls off" a branch to land in the womb of an earthly being, or in a seed to grow in a garden or forest.

The details of any temporal lifetime are known in the spirit realm but are filtered through the Great Tree, and only some of them become interfused into the emerging consciousness of a human newly-born into the three-dimensional world. Some of the knowledge that may accompany an individual at the conscious or shallow subconscious levels might include some details of the family born into, certain circumstances of the life's environment, and the awareness of spiritual tasks assigned while in the spirit realm to be carried out in the physical.

The degree of forgetfulness experienced by a spirit being is not controlled by the Great Tree and is unique to each individual, as is the recovery of those memories. It is the desire and ability of the individual to live a life according to the Will of God that will allow the individual to recover memories of their true and complete existence. Even so, knowledge will only be given as it is necessary to the execution of The Great Plan. The fact that you are reading these words now, in this time and place, is evidence that you are strong enough to assist in The Great Plan in these last few years.

***

The interfusion of Life from the Great Tree is set within a supernatural field of which the exact details are known and controlled only by God's Will, therefore it is impossible to attempt to psychically enter the Great Tree to obtain information about oneself or any other being. There is no tampering with the perfection of what it does or how it operates. The one thing that is known absolutely about all beings in physical form is that by way of The Tree, a network of passages for God's Will has been created within the temple that is your body. This circuitry is vital to the transmission of life for all beings everywhere. All life is inter-related and part of The One Body of God.

The River of Life

In *Volume 1*, Mary spoke of allowing an atom to split on its own accord instead of using human thought and effort to produce the result. She was hinting at what happens when a being looks beyond the confines of this three-dimensional world, and chooses instead to follow the flow of the River of Life. When the sacred waters of Jehovah Rapha are claimed as a living reality, an explosion of healing occurs within the life of one entrapped in the world mind. Health is the natural state of *hozhoni*, and the explosion brings balance. Harmony flows through those who continue to love God in thought, word, and action.

The River of Life connects your spirit to the Great Tree, and you are the one who will determine the strength of that connection. The power of this link is contained within you, and consists of the very thoughts which you, the spirit being made human, directly control.

It is true that the flow of life force for all beings everywhere has been disrupted by negative thought and action, but now you have been reminded of your wonderful and natural place here and it is time for you to radiate goodness from your place within the Great Tree. True healing reaches far above and beyond the physical.

The moment you come back to the absolute truth that you belong to God, acknowledging that there is only one God who adores and loves you eternally, you are permanently healed. Do this once as a pure and sincere offering, and the spiritual healing is complete.

FROM ELISE'S DIARY

It has been more than twenty years since the occurrence of miracles became an everyday reality for me, and there is no end to the diverse, abundant, and often-unpredictable healing experiences that have been witnessed by these eyes I use.

All of the healings—personal, social, global, spiritual, and cosmic—have been amazing to behold over the course of time, but time can be an illusion, as well as a great inconvenience. Time exists only in this temporal, mundane plane, but attachment to it and the belief that it determines the life experience, complicates the vision of what healing is, as the healing is happening. In addition, people have no control over any aspect of their healings, however much that is desired. Some healings are immediate, some are postponed, and some seem never to happen at all.

Being witness to the immediate physical healings of people and animals has been a wondrous gift. It is these kinds of miraculous healings that are the most impressive, as a physical healing is unquestionable because of the first-person quality of the experience. When cancerous tumors are miraculously lifted from a person, in the name of God, this tends to produce in many minds a state of awe. And why shouldn't it? Being immediately freed from a physical condition of pain or suffering is certainly something to rejoice over and is not a daily occurrence. I have never encountered one individual who received a physical healing who did not then return to God in devotion. It seems that God gives physical healings so that hope, belief, and faith in God will radiate to all others in that person's life. The wonders of God should be expressed so that they may touch the lives of everyone.

It is saddening however, to have observed mental healings take years, if not a lifetime, to be accepted, welcomed,
and integrated as real into the personal life so that a new
existence may be put into practice. Watching loved ones
battle within themselves over a psychological issue or life
experience is difficult. No matter how much I may truly
love someone in purity, I have never been able to make
that person see the light.

Without the personal dedication to give all to God,
the emotional thinking of the ego will always return to
keep one trapped in the suffering of illusory negative perceptions of painful circumstances in the past, no matter
how much a person strives to believe that the past does
not exist.

It only takes once to give all of the past away to God. I
know this absolutely and beyond the shadow of a doubt
to be true. God arranged it to be so, but this truth is
denied, rejected, or fought by so many — a self-defeating
and destructive behavior here on Earth that is most perplexing and saddening and entirely unnecessary.

A person need only ask God once to take all the past, all
the negative thoughts, and all the mental suffering away,
and it is done immediately. God transmutes all negative
energy upon first request, so long as the individual seeking
the mental release acknowledges that God exists. This
is the most important kind of healing. It is permanent,
and it is far more powerful and real than anything of the
world, or the suffering itself.

I am not a slave to ego. I wish I could use the force of
the very love that courses through me to blast its doings
all away, but that would be going against God's Will.
Each beautiful person on this planet must learn to see
through ego and put it in its place for themselves. Each
beautiful spirit being here is a vital part of this Great

Plan, and it is upsetting to me that billions of people just don't understand.

Ego is devious in nature and will repeatedly tell the suffering human being that they are never done with painful past issues or circumstances. Once a thought of this kind is placed within a conscious mind and allowed to remain there, that thought can easily become a kind of energetic entity and be given power over the individual's life. The end result is the belief that emotional thinking is just a part of the person that cannot be removed, or worse yet, it has become a part of human nature.

If only humanity would remember that the conscious mind is simply the level of the mind that holds all that is learned and imprinted by the self, from the family, and from the world at large. One big mental download could trash much of it without any ill effect to the person oppressed by it. Emotional thinking is a learned reaction to life circumstances involving other humans. It is the fuel that feeds both the conscious mind and the ego. Ego is the identity of form, assigned by way of the Great Tree, but when on Earth, ego is shaped by the growing mind's reactions, expressed by way of the conscious mind.

None of these elements — ego, emotion, and mind — can exist in isolation, and yet each tries to make itself the most important. Ego is shaped by emotional reactions and given expression by the conscious mind, generating a deadly but widely-embraced illusion in today's world cultures. This is the major disease affecting the world at large.

The purity of true-life consciousness, which is communion with God, is what was given to this world by the Founders, millions of years ago as the cornerstone of a blessed experiment for a new species and its civilization. *Hozhoni* was the breathing essence of the origins of this planet, as well as its promise. Many people are disconnected from this and suffering because of it.

Humanity has never taught the children of this world the truth that all belong to God, because the acts of teaching and learning require embracing that which is being professed. The look of belonging to God has never been truly modeled by any generation of this world, and thus the fact that all people are actually spirit beings has been almost entirely lost from the collective human consciousness. Coinciding with this, too many adults have displayed the belief that emotional thinking is part of human nature as they see it, thus increasing the disconnection of the conscious mind from spirit.

As a human participating in this of kind of disconnected world, great strength is needed to put the conscious mind and ego in proper control. Requesting this strength from God's mercy is the only way to break through the spiritual and mental lies, so as to welcome the human life birthed into that of the spirit being.

A human's ultimate purpose is to be a pure vessel for God's Will, so that the body, the conscious mind, and the ego, are inter-fused with the frequencies of God. To really know that you belong to, and love God first of all, is to also love the self, which should be the same as love for all humans. This is the *hozhoni* to which Din was referring. It is pure bliss, pure harmony, and pure heaven on Earth. It makes a body feel good, and it's free.

But for the individual stuck in the warfare of the disconnected mind, it is a self-created hell. As this mental battle of conscious mind and ego is being waged, the individual will believe that their process of healing may not be working or is even non-existent. Some may deny that healing is for them because the negative doings of the past cannot be forgiven. Some may believe that their faith in the greater power of God is too weak, and that lack of attainment or denial of healing is their punishment for that.

What is true is that this kind of fallacious thinking creates energetic blocks for the individual, making them unable to recognize healing in its minute and subtle forms, or preventing them from receiving any healing at all. If belief in and attachment to the voices of the conscious mind are allowed, then moments turn into days, weeks, months, and possibly even years, with no real healing having occurred. This kind of battle is far too common. So many people leave their bodies feeling disheartened and weak after years of being broken by the stories of their lives. This kind of illusion creates a gap between mind and spirit, leaving them as limbs severed from the Will of God.

God will not punish people for human weakness if they still see themselves as trapped by the same old stuff after they have given their troubles to God. God knows each and every affliction, each and every pain, each and every iniquity, but has already removed them all. It is people who keep bringing them back.

God is Perfection and the only Origin and Source of Unconditional Love. Just as it is impossible for God to create suffering, it is also impossible for God to punish those children who suffer.

Well said, Daughter.

Mother!

Now explain what happened to you last night, and do not leave out any details. It is vital that you describe the consequences of bringing a negative entity into ones mind. Humanity must go deeper in its understanding of how dark thoughts bring forth dark things from the other side into

the personal and collective life of all.

I always have to take a moment when Mother appears from out of nowhere like that with such a direct message. The degree of intensity varies widely depending on what she wants to convey. It is not a simple thing for her to come to Earth in full form, for her powerful presence is more than this world can bear. I have come to realize what I have experienced of her Earth visitations have only been a fragment of her total being. I have tried to share this with you, but she is so much bigger than life.

I am not sure if what happened last night can be called a dream, a vision, or a nightmare. It was definitely a personal healing for me, and then some. I know I was not asleep—at least not in the conventional sense, and I did not intentionally bring forth any part of it whatsoever. It hit me hard. Actually, worse than hard I spent the entire night feeling my bones, ligaments, and tendons being squeezed clean of ego thought-filth, and horrid circumstances from my past in this lifetime. The result was a physical clearing, a mental cleansing, and a cosmic message about something horrid, all in one night with an ending that was absolutely blessed.

I wanted to take a bath that evening to relax, as my muscles were cramped from writing on the computer all day. Normally, I would have done some yoga postures beforehand as part of my weekend ritual, but there was something different in store for me having nothing to do with relaxation. I decided to skip the yoga and headed straight for the bathtub.

I put a cupful of Epsom salts into the steaming hot water and a few drops of lavender and chamomile essential oil. I was alone in the mostly quiet house, as my two children were visiting their grandparents for the weekend. The only sounds were the running water and my daughter's pet mouse spinning the wheel in its cage. I wanted total quiet and peace, so I twisted the water on with a little more force to drown out all other sounds. The aroma of the lavender and chamomile helped my mind sink into the bliss of the wet heat.

Suddenly, the soothing floral and herbal fragrance was overpowered by the stench of cigarette smoke. I do not smoke, nor do I allow others to engage in that addiction while in my home, nonetheless, the smell was quite strong. I jolted upright in alarm.

I listened carefully for a minute or two but heard no sounds of intruders. I decided to proceed with my bath and lay back in the tub, even though my sense of unease continued. I watched the wispy steam rise from the cold porcelain as the bathtub continued to fill with hot water. There was no logical explanation for the smell of smoke accompanied by the scratchy feeling in my nose and throat and the stinging in my eyes as if it were being blown directly into my face. In spite of my inclination to hold my breath, I began to breathe deeply—I had come to realize that I was about to experience yet another unpredictable spiritual travel adventure.

I spoke a prayer. "Whatever this is about, O Holy One, I throw myself into You. It is always and only You that I breathe, so do with me now whatever You will."

I slid deeper into the tub, submerging my head in the water in an effort to escape the stench. My ears filled with the liquid warmth and my heart began to beat faster. The discomfort of my eyes, nose, and throat increased to the level of pain as the fiery smell filled my neck, sternum, and upper back. The vertebra at the top of my spine felt like it was about to explode. The ribs around my heart felt like they were being squeezed. The sensations intensified and I began to feel fear, as well. Everywhere that my body did not feel the pressure and pain seemed not to exist.

I kept my eyes closed tight in order to maintain control of my commitment to surrender to God in this experience. It was the only thing I could do to get through this bewildering trial.

I thought the squeezing of my bones and the fire ripping through my cells was caused by some destructive energy piercing my flesh, but then images from my past were brought to my mind. My tears of pain and fear changed to tears of grief and remorse as I relived scenes from my life long ago, acted out in unwholesome places with immature people whom I used to think of as friends.

The vision took the form of a parade of the faces of people I had trusted deeply in my post-adolescent years. They were the people I had embraced within a particular community which claimed to love "Great Spirit," but whose behaviors spoke otherwise in the end. I saw clearly the faces of those to whom I had given a huge chunk of my life and heart, and who had latter shown themselves to have negative and even evil intentions toward me. I had spent a great deal of time with these people over the course of years, talking at length about living wild in nature, around campfires under the light of the full moon. I had revealed very private things to these people, and had not realized, until that moment in the bathtub, just how much damage had been done.

Just when I thought it would not get any worse, it did. The vision shifted and the scene intensified. I watched as what can only be described as a dark energy of hellish origin poured over the Earth in a massive wave of fire.

The stench of smoke then turned into the smell of decay, and joined with the fury of the burning in my heart and body. I watched as people screamed foul words while their own brains exploded. I saw murders, rape, and fires that burned whole cities down to smoldering ash. I saw millions of people lying prostrate at the feet of the political leaders standing before them. I watched as those leaders morphed into a single living form radiating negativity and wearing the garb of one who has great power and authority in society. It smiled, and from its smile came wordless lies that spread like a vile, energetic cloud over the millions of human beings that bowed before it.

As the cloud descended on the throngs of people, it began to suck the very life force from them, feeding the stolen life-essence to the many-faced figure of authority, filling it with dark unnatural power. I saw the malevolent being as a frantic, desperate, lustful creature of many faces, enjoying the power it drew from so many.

The network of light surrounding the figure and the millions who lay before it, was also affected by the vile energy, becoming a ragged, convoluted, chaotic vision of disfigured shapes with terrible wounds. Gaping holes appearing in the network emanated the hollow sense of absolute nothingness. That was the most frightening part of my entire vision as that nothingness seemed to be what the humanoid of many faces was craving.

I sensed that the goal of the humanoid was to engulf all of the people on this planet and drag them into the nothingness. The goal was total annihilation of life, and it was proceeding rapidly and with great success, as more and more human beings were falling victim with every breath of the dark humanoid.

The vision shifted again, and I could see myself. I stood rigid, both hands at the back of my neck, with fingers interlocking. I saw my body as a grid of crystal golden light standing within a much larger, all-consuming white-gold radiance, so brilliant that it illumined the world for miles around. I saw myself begin to approach the humanoid creature.

My flesh was shaking uncontrollably in the bathwater while I was in this vision. I was aware and wide-awake simultaneously in both the spiritual and the mundane dimensions. I knew I was doing exactly what I was supposed to be doing, but there was really nothing of me there at all.

I walked towards the dark figure—who was now more of a formless entity than a man—inhaling deeply and pursing my lips as I neared it. A deep and long Hum rose from my throat as my eyes locked firmly onto its forehead. It had been rocking back and forth as it loomed over the millions of people who were now gasping in their worship of it. The moment it felt the Hum, it looked up, catching sight of the radiant force of the Hum that now filled whole of the area. The purity of this force shot through every particle, every wave, and every cell of each being in the scene. Many now lay lifeless on the ground, but there were others who had been brought back into health and wholeness, by the living vibration of the Hum that was creating a beautiful unearthly Glow.

The force of the Hum had washed through the whole of the scene with one clean sweep of brilliant light, annihilating the vile energy produced by the entity. Only a white-gold radiance remained—intense, pure light.

I opened my eyes. The bathwater had cooled to lukewarm. My body cracked and popped as I moved those muscles and joints that had been compressed and burned by the energies of the vision. My head felt weightless, as if the heavy loads I had carried for many years had been lifted from me. In their stead, I had been entrusted with a new and terrifying awareness.

I realized that my fingers were still interlaced at the back of my neck, as they had been when I faced the evil entity of the vision. I separate them slowly, then pressed the tips deep into the spaces between bone and flesh, feeling and hearing tiny pops and crackles from my skull. Energy shot through my neck, down my spine, and up out my head, and for a while I seemed not to breathe at all. I was riding in the Spirit of God. I wanted to stay in that moment for eternity, but my own spirit confirmed in my mind, that my wish was already a reality.

I took a deep breath and noticed that the stench was completely gone. In its place I could smell the scent of the Jasmine flower, my favorite. I murmured a brief prayer of thanks.

I stepped out of the bath, wrapped myself in my robe, and headed for my bedroom. I was ready for the rest of my sleepless night.

As I lay in bed, I became aware of changes in my physical body. The arthritic condition which had been plaguing my upper back, neck, and shoulders for some time was now gone, and my breath moved through and out of my body with ease. Years of negativity had just been lifted from every cell of my flesh.

I stared up at the ceiling over my bed where the Hectaran System is mapped out with glow-in-the-dark, stick-on stars. The last thing I saw before I drifted off to sleep was the Glow of Home, and my last thought was, *Thank you.*

Christa's Story

The workmen had gone for the day, and Christa was alone in the entry to the old parlor that was under renovation. It was six weeks into her job as the company artist, and she had six more weeks left in her contract with the owner of Nene's, this expensive new Italian restaurant.

The man who owned it was her *zio*, an uncle-figure who was not directly related to her but who had been an important part of her life ever since Christa could remember. Tony Cavarrci, a man with strong business savvy and a huge Italian body, had given Christa the freedom to display her artistic perfection in an unusually generous amount of time. It was the last three months of the countdown to the restaurant's grand opening. Expectations for Nene's were high, based on the well-publicized reputation of its top chef from Sicily. He had been persuaded—and funded—by Tony to relocate to the Heartland of America and make a little piece of Italy come to life there. Christa felt the need for perfection in her work, but while a chef can assemble a masterpiece in a few hours, her work would require a whole season.

Zio Tony had given Christa her own key to the restaurant and permission to work during whatever hours of the evening and night she chose. She made it a point to come to the restaurant well after the construction workers had left. She did not seek attention from men, or from anyone. She had chosen to immerse herself in her artistic gift as a means of rejecting the negative behaviors of the world she observed around her. The only thing pure, and the only thing that gave her true comfort and solace, was what was conveyed through her hands to the paintbrush.

Christa looked at her watch as she fumbled for her keys. It was about seven o'clock in the evening.

She took stock of where she was in the mural painting, seeing the whole of the piece in her mind, even before she walked through the door. The last interaction Christa had had with her *zio* Tony, a month and a half ago, came back to her as she unlocked the side door. She smiled at the recollection.

"Don't push this easy street I am paving for you, little girl. Your daddy was like a brother to me, and I have watched you grow up with your paints all over your face. Just get the job done in time, *capiche*? And remember, you're still gonna be waiting tables, right? I know that the money I am giving you for this mural could set up your I.R.A, but you still want the waitress job, right?"

"I get it, *Zio*. Don't worry. You know I only let the best come through. And, yes, I want to do tables here when it opens. I got bills to pay, too, you know." Christa's smile laid the whole matter to rest.

Christa laughed at the memory as she walked into the dimly lit construction zone, feeling for the switch to turn on the floodlights that illuminated her workspace.

Christa loved silence. She adored the late-night hours when the restaurant was empty of people and filled with nothing but the space for her creative spirit. She viewed the mural wall with discriminating eyes and allowed her breath to welcome the focus of peace. She never began any painting without making absolutely sure she was over-whelmed with peace. If not, she could not and would not paint. Serenity was the fuel that allowed the creative spirit to consume her mind and to command through her hands the outpouring of creativity into form and color.

Christa had not learned how to paint from a single individual, nor had she ever attended any art school. She was a natural master. In the prior three years, and by no willful activity on her part, many opportunities to sell her works had been made manifest. She looked at this abundance as simply a by-product of the artistic spirit running through her, commanding her mind and body, and she never questioned why the demands for her paintings seemed to suddenly appear.

At first, it was a few local businessmen who had connections with Tony, but then well-known companies and even a few national organizations had requested her paintings, offering handsome sums of money for her creations. Christa had always chosen to demand anonymity, accepting the money, but never spreading her own name.

The C.E.O. of a major bank in St. Louis, upon acceptance of her three-foot by four-foot portrayal of Lewis and Clark with Sacajawea, said, "I have to ask you why you don't sign your name to your works? I heard this was your habit, but I insist that you sign this painting. I want to tell everyone I know about you."

Christa's reply was, "No, thank you. I will not do that. If it's a problem for you, I will happily give you a refund."

"Why do they all have to ask me why?" Christa thought, smiling as she placed the check for payment in her wallet.

Christa shook her head. It was time to get back to the task at hand. She glanced at her wristwatch, noticing that nearly thirty minutes had passed while she daydreamed. She huffed in disapproval, readied her palette, and prepared to make the final touches on the toes of the "olive-basket woman" on the enormous wall.

She kept glancing up at the face of the woman, then down at her palette. The image of the woman was thrilling to her, and yet she felt an inner remorse because the figure was almost finished.

Feeling a bit out of sorts as a result of her emotion, Christa began to dab and mix, mix and dab, completely unsatisfied with the color combination she was producing.

She looked up at the woman's legs, then, with another huff, scraped blobs of paint off into her bucket of rejected paint slop. She felt an unusual air of discontent. Her thoughts began again, and in her frustration, she spoke them aloud. "What is wrong with me tonight? Something's not right about those toes. They're too yellowish. She's got to be perfect. What do I need to do? I need to make this absolutely perfect."

Her attention was divided between the frantic movements of her brush in one hand and the squeezing of paint tubes in the other when a voice penetrated her consciousness. "One need not do anything but love God with all of one's being, just as you do with the painting, Christa." The rich feminine Italian voice spoke with as much vividness as the painting itself.

Christa stared into the eyes of the woman whose face had been the first image to be born on the blank white wall. She was entranced and in communion with the energy radiating from the woman's eyes, and her body tightened with surprise as she sensed something impossible was starting to happen.

"Do not be so alarmed, Christa. You know that I have been with you, speaking to you from the inside for the whole of your life, but you are only now ready to receive me in a new way, *cara mia*."

The colors of the image came out of the wall like a gust of summer breeze, except that this dynamic stream of energy was composed of all the hues of the paints Christa had used. They swirled away in a clockwise motion, leaving the wall completely blank—which was more alarming to Christa at that moment than the supernatural activity itself. She concentrated on the fact that the body of painted light was taking actual physical form, and the image of the woman was being made complete right in front of her.

Dressed in her simple long-sleeved cotton blouse and a blue-gray skirt that fell to her mid-calf, the woman, still holding her basket, now stood before Christa as real as life.

"What, in the name of ..." She wasn't sure if she was going crazy, or if this apparition was as real as the oil paint stains that had found permanence on most of her clothing.

She slowly laid her brush on her palette and said to the impossible woman, "Umm, hello. Who are you?"

The beautiful woman laughed lovingly. "*Il mia cara*, you know exactly who I am."

Christa was suddenly overwhelmed by a wave of warmth, purity, and nourishment such as she had never experienced. She began to reply, but amazement and doubt muddled her thoughts like the chaotic hues of paint she had discarded only moments before.

"Nonna? Grandma? It that you? How is this possible? I don't think I am feeling so hot right now. I think I need to go home."

"Christa! By the love of God that makes you who you are, be still and be with me now."

Christa sat down immediately on the chair behind her, shoved there gently by an unseen force. She looked up with rapt attention and awe into the face of the radiant woman who appeared exactly as she had been painted. She had spent three weeks perfecting the face, and then another three weeks on her body. Absolutely nothing but this woman had been the focus of Christa's artistic spirit for an entire month and a half, and now here she was, conversing with ... her grandmother, who had just emerged from a flat batch of smeared, colored grease on a wall.

Christa wiped her hair from her face, leaving a streak of yellow paint smeared across her forehead.

"Dear Christa. You are just as messy as you have always

been." Nonna approached and wiped the paint from the artist's sweating brow with the hem of her skirt.

"Are you ready to listen, Christa?" Nonna was staring into Christa's eyes with indescribable intensity. The sensation of it was so consuming that she trembled for a moment, holding on to the wooden chair for stability.

"Yes, I welcome you here, Nonna. I guess. I am sorry. Am I okay, though? Am I dead? What is going on? How did you …?"

Nonna pulled up a chair, placed Christa's left hand into her lap, and replied, "Oh, there is so much, *cara mia*, so much that you will come to remember. But first, no, you are not dead. You are very much alive, more so than you have ever been."

"I am sorry, Nonna. I just don't know what is happening right now. I need to——" Christa passed out, falling into the lap of her loving great-great-grandmother.

When she came back into consciousness a few moments later, Christa was staring up into the face of her beautiful grandmother, who was still there with her, in the flesh.

"You need to listen and to welcome me here, cara mia. That is all you need to do for right now," Nonna said gently while petting Christa's forehead. "You asked just a moment ago, what it is you need to do. I heard you myself. This world does not know how to love, Christa, so what you must do is teach them. Show them, through the work of your paintbrush, what the essence of this love is. This is what you need to do to make it perfect."

"But I already give my paintings all that I am, Nonna. And there's nothing much of me in them. It is what comes through me, into the paintings, that is the perfection."

Nonna smiled. "Then why were you so upset with my toes, eh?"

Christa had no words.

"*Cara mia*, I am not talking about the perfection of your creative spirit. You have already put yourself into communion with this. Your work now is to return your creations back to the Will that is beyond your own. There is little time left for all of them to wake up, Christa. I want you to paint into this world the purpose of why you are here. If you paint this now, you will be making the most perfect masterpiece. And all who gaze upon it will behold in wonder, and will be healed."

"Huh?"

For the first time in her life, Christa felt at a complete loss. She could see nothing of herself, yet she could feel a kind of force beginning to overwhelm the whole of her body. Nonna's words were washing through her, and Christa's spirit was merging with something much more powerful than anything she had ever felt before.

Christa lifted herself up from Nonna's lap, full of joy. In less than a second, she had come to realize why she had wanted to remain secretive about herself in relation to her art all these years. She was being filled with a new kind of Glow, which she would be compelled to portray with paint in the near future.

"Oh my God," she said, ecstatic with the radiant clarity of everything Nonna had just given her—in words, and in communion with Spirit. Christa was reborn in that very moment and without question. She knew that to be a fact.

"Oh, Nonna, thank you. Thank God. Now I know what I have been leaving out. Now I know Who I have been forgetting. I get it, Nonna. I am on fire with this gift!"

As Christa spoke these last words, her eyes became illuminated beyond the spark of mere creativity, with the flame of unconditional love.

"Nonna, I love you, but you have to get back into the wall, now. I have to start painting. I am ready." Christa smiled, thinking how silly that statement had sounded.

"Yes, you are ready, Christa." Nonna rose from her chair smiling. "You must now finish my toes."

Christa looked down at Nonna's feet. Where the left foot was finished with five finely drawn toes, the right foot culminated in a blurred mass of yellow.

They laughed, and the beloved grandmother embraced her dearest great-grandchild.

"Are you going to have to undo yourself now and turn back into all my swirling paints again, Nonna?"

"No, my dear, I can never undo myself, for now I breathe in more ways than you know—because of you. Just remember one thing." Nonna stepped onto the ledge nearest the mural.

"What's that, Nonna?"

"Open yourself to embrace those who walk the Truth. They will find you again. You will know them very soon."

Nonna walked into the wall, placing herself in the exact position and form that had been born of Christa's spirit in communion with God.

Christa painted through the night, with a new sense of power and awareness that had been lacking just a few hours before. She stopped only at the first sounds of the construction workers returning through the back door.

ANNIE'S THOUGHTS ON
THE ART OF THE IN-BETWEEN

True visual artists like Christa know the power of the "in-between", and they practice their artistic gifts enough to make a mastery of translating this realm of life into the subject that appears on their canvases. True painters, sculptors, and others committed to God's vision know how to make their eyes see through the lines of worldly life in order to receive the rays of inspiration from God, making this knowledge and wisdom available for those in the world who are in need of such cleansing, nurturing, and nourishment. When one observes these kinds of rare artistic creations, there is no conscious analysis of His Spirit's transmission. It is readily felt and known within the very life force of the observer. It is another form of God's blessings within the third dimension.

These blessed artistic beings work hard every moment of their lives to radiate God coming through them for the good of all who would receive. They know by way of an added sense how awesome God is, and they want what God wants: for all beings to come back to this kind of life.

True artists are healers radiating God's Will, and they are very few and far between upon your planet right now. I can count them on two hands.

One does not have to be a masterful visual artist, however, to do wonderful things, and to assist in The Great Plan. Reconnecting with the bounties offered by pure life is reward enough for a heart returned to God. The degree to which you let go of your worldly sight, which is nothing more than the thoughts that you had fossilized into a mica-thin mind, is the degree to which you begin to receive fruits from God. You cannot, however, just give your thoughts away and be done with it. You must, with the spirit of a warrior, saturate

127

your mind with all that is contained in this and in the other volumes of this series. You must choose to breathe Truth in every moment and allow the Unconditional Love — that radiance that makes up the life you share with all — to command your life.

Elise's Vision: A Mystery Ride into Heaven and Healing

I love her so much it hurts. There are galaxies exploding because of my aching for her to be in my arms. But it only hurts when I am making myself stuck in a place of sorrow, of anguish, over things I cannot control. Most of the time my love for her is beyond full, so impossibly huge, and it keeps getting bigger. She knows how I have struggled in this lifetime, and still she keeps on laughing, laughing, laughing. I cannot separate myself from her, nor can she from me. Yet because we are in two different realms, assigned to separate tasks for now, there are moments when the mind I am now using thinks she is so far away. Coupled with the fact that this body has only recently healed enough to fully receive my spirit, to be awakened into the Truth of who I am, there have been illusory gaps of wondering why all of my beloveds seemed so far away.

There was nothing worthy in the mental addiction to lies that I had embraced, so it was into the blue-green fire of God's Love that I cast myself. Through each and every breath I belong to You, timelessly. This is my eternal reality. This is my true nature.

I am not a saint. I never loved myself out of ego, nor had I ever chosen willfully to rise above my past. It was impossible to think that I could do this alone, as I had tried all the positive affirmations I could conjure, hoping to just blip myself away from the darkness of mind. It never worked, and the lightning came through strong enough to awaken me to how the biggest wolf in sheep's clothing was the doing of my own ideation.

I am being breathed by the only One who adores all of

life. I am being thrust into this most perfect of journeys, being prepared for what is about to emerge.

In this very moment, I am looking up, out, here, there, and beyond into a starry expanse that has no end. This part of space is pure black with shimmering diamond stars that are mesmerizingly bright in their light. They are all humming their own perfect, synchronous part of the cosmos. They are ever-changing, ever-dancing, ever-filling space with their own unique perfection. These are the Star Beings who receive positive thought from this Earth and cast it back and through the universe. They are not as plentiful as they once were millions of years ago when Annica was new-born, but some of them are still here, working in communion with the Great Tree and the Creation Frequency. They are the ancestors of the star-nations of the human physiology, and they are far beyond. Their shine makes me cry in awe and wonder of their love for humanity, in their love for the original vision of this species. They have never lost faith.

It is unfolding. The Return has begun.

I hear the sound of hooves stampeding across a starry sky. The riders of the horses approach. The shaking of the cosmos reverberates through my heart—it is the sound of my blood, and I am lost within the ecstasy of it all. The stars barely able to contain themselves, knowing that the ceremony in honor of the completion of a particular mission of devotion is about to occur. Stars are good at being patient when it comes to mysteries being revealed. They are able to wait a very long time for God to unleash the flood in the most perfect of moments. We shall celebrate one moment in particular, which has been prepared for millennia. There will be great rejoicing indeed.

There now comes into my sight a Glowing star who,

with waves like a crystal ocean, reaches for me. It is dancing with exuberance and a display of snowflake artistry, with intricate, rapidly changing patterns. It is speaking to me in geometric forms of supernatural beauty. I take a moment to process the vibrations coming through me. They remind me to understand that I have worked diligently in so many lifetimes. They want me to honor the fact that I kept a glimmer of their work alive through each life of my own. They want me to rejoice in my place in communion with them.

The Riders travel swiftly. They are closer, closer, and now there is the sound of the ancestors' song carried with the pounding of horses' hooves. Their voices are streams of fire, water, air, and starry life force jetting forth into this moment, through every molecule of space.

Earth opens up, releasing the mysteries of the grandmothers' and grandfathers' songs, sunk deep into the soils for so long, back to their spirits coming across the skies.

The Riders number in the hundreds. The one I have been waiting for is at the front, hair blowing divine energy in the dust of her starry sprint. She has summoned my horse for me, and it is a homecoming long overdue.

I leap to the back of my horse, whom I call White Beauty, and I lean over to kiss this other smiling spirit being whom I adore. She reaches out to enfold me in her embrace. The universe waits for our holy holding of each other to be completed in this way. A great sigh spreads throughout the realm of God. We begin to ride across the universe to our destination

There is no talking. There is only the pulse pounding of hooves in harmony with the ancestors' songs. There is one unified heart, and the celebration begins. It is a supernatural feast, indeed, as the songs rush forth through each and every being, each and every star, filling and satiating all with the Presence of God.

My horse rears up in exaltation—a display of praise and worship for God. It has been such a long time since White Beauty has carried me and her joy is uncontainable. I hold on with ease, calling her name to calm her a bit. She responds instantly, stomping her lightning hooves and whinnying in obedience. Ah, my White Beauty, whose real name if spoken, would destroy the network of life on Earth with the sheer force of her love.

It is good to be with the riders of the horses, but especially with this other spirit being.

She rides beside me, at time leaning low over the outstretched neck of her mount, then rising to stand tiptoed on the back of her own blessed spirit horse. She swoops down into her horse's body, becoming one with its energy, pulsing and pounding harder and faster. I follow suit, in communion with the bodies of our blessed sisters, these horses who are so dear to us.

We stream back at will into our spirit forms, regaining the shape of our feminine bodies. We laugh as color beings flow joyfully into our bodies. The whole universe is showered with our intended goodness as we ride. Doing nothing in isolation, we are intent on everything that advances the perfection of The Great Plan. We can see and feel how the joy of our being together accelerates The Great Plan, as is our intention. Together, our burning purity casts down fire through all of life, cleansing that which needs cleansing, nourishing that which needs nourishing, and removing that which must be removed. It is none of our doing, but it is all accomplished with the strength drawn through our communion in God.

We ride on, and the purpose of our celebration is revealed. We approach the realm of a sun that is about to leave its form, to become a supernova, as it is now ready to move on to its next assignment. It is so very far away from Earth—billions of light years—but it has been assisting humanity for millions of years. It has been radiating its own life force to support life on Earth and in many other star systems, as well.

We have come to thank it, to bless it, and to be a part of the explosion that will return it to the Great Tree, Who is waiting to take it in.

The legions pause for a moment around this sun, one of billions in this particular universe. It had chosen to take upon itself the work of transforming negative energy from Earth. This sun has been using its own unseen rays to draw out all of the negative thought and activity from the Earth's dimension and carry the filth away from the solar system and the Milky Way galaxy. The valiant star acted further to direct the energy away from the Great Tree, and to separate itself from the other suns so that it could safely and properly transmute the darkness into usable vibrations of goodness to be disseminated throughout the universe.

This work was specific and focused for millions of years but is now complete. This sun has completed its own life cycle within the Will of The All, and there is nothing more for the sun to do in its current form.

We begin to sing praises. The sun hears its cue, and we witness the Glow of millions of years of loving and burning for God's Will coming to fruition. The center of the sun begins to layer itself into folds of red, orange, gold, green, blue, silver, purple, rose, and more too exquisite to name and impossible to describe—folding and weaving, rising and falling into intricate kaleidoscopic geometries.

The sun begins its final explosion with small eruptions of exuberant delight. It tells us of the joy our presence brings, and of its gratitude to us for the millions of years of our prayer and support for its life and mission. It sends a special burst of its blessing to each of our hundreds of individual spirit-being bodies. We are mesmerized by the doings of God.

My sweet one draws closer to me, nudging her face into my neck, as she leans over her horse. I pull her tight to me, as we prepare for the final moment.

We watch as the explosions increase in intensity and frequency, resulting not in a fallout of deadly radiation but in a shower of God's Love for us and for all who are willing to receive it. Stars are shaken. Some are destroyed in the purposeful plan of their own passing, having been lieutenants under the direction of the valiant star. Other stars grow in size with a newly-born effervescence, for the dying sun has bequeathed its ancient wisdom and distributed its acquired knowledge to all its blessed star family as far and wide as God can reach.

The fallout from the exploding sun reaches to Earth, bringing healing to humans, releasing multitudes from their cancers, chronic diseases, and deadly viruses that have contaminated their fleshly vessels. Many humans harbor dark thoughts and plans for destruction. The supernova will bring healing and cleansing to them, as well. Everyone everywhere will be affected in some way.

Those who receive this gift with gratitude and acknowledgment of its Source, are blessed beyond words.

I am being told to stop—All medicine has its proper dose. Give the healing time to settle in.

Welcome Home.

Din Explains More About the In-Between

Annie wants me to make a point before continuing any further in this volume. All three volumes of Mary's Diary contain key words and phrases—codes that will not only awaken the readers more quickly to the knowledge of their destiny, but will also generate healing within the bodies, minds, and spirits of those readers. By studying these volumes, you will be preparing yourself to receive the blessings and healing described in them. This book is a book of blessing and healing. Call it magic if you wish, but that is not what it is. It is the healing energy from above being gifted to those who have demonstrated the faith necessary to read up to this point in the Diary.

Annie touched on the topic of the *in-between* previously in these pages, and it is something that must be thoroughly addressed, as true healing does not work within time, but comes from the place between the dimensions where God manipulates the elements in order to direct specific penetrating healing frequencies to individual beings.

The ancient Celtic concept of the *in-between* has been described as the *space between the spaces where magic is made to happen.*

Although the ancient Celts had hit upon one of the great Truths of God, they did it in a rather haphazard way. In that day and age they simply did not have the awareness of the Truth that is available now. By the time the Celts began to wonder about where things really came from, much damage had been done by man-made philosophies and religions, and human beings were incapable of operating with true mental wisdom and clarity. All one has to do is to look at the chaotic mess of contemporary human culture to see the truth of that statement. True Wisdom is simply not present on Earth today, apart from the teachings of Christ. In addition, there is an expanding anti-God culture in which True Wisdom has been replaced by the unrestricted, self-serving, rambling thoughts of the wants, wishes, and desires of people all over this globe. Even common sense has been tossed out in favor of bizarre, so-called progressive political fabrications designed to enslave the populace and make it impossible to achieve higher wisdom of any nature.

The Celts believed that their magic came from places that exist between places — the brief time when day turns to night, the boundary where a field of flowers turns abruptly into a forest, the doorway created by two trees bending toward each other over a path. Dozens of these manifestations of the *in-between* governed many of the activities of the ancient Celtic culture. Much of their religion, as well as their politics, were specifically designed to accommodate interaction with and within these *in-between* places.

What Annie wants me to clarify for you here, is that while there was much logic behind what the Celts practiced, the motive for their practice was incorrect. They were motivated primarily by fear and superstition. Many would not even pass through a "nature door" of trees for fear of never coming out again. Nature and the gods were not to be merely respected — they were to be feared. The *in-between* places were portals leading to dark, mysterious places where only the gods were allowed to tread. A person had to be very careful even approaching these magical entrances into the unknown.

Among the things that Christ brought when He came to Earth was clarity concerning many things that had become confused in the minds of humans. Of greatest import, He made it clear that the Creator is not a God to be feared, but One to be loved and worshiped. Jesus replaced the ancient superstitions and suspicions with a religion that contained a relationship with God, as well as the promise of a Heavenly Realm beyond the imaginings of mankind.

Annie is urging me to consult with Elise before I continue further with the discussion of the *in-between*. I've been trying to reach her for the last five hours, but she's not answering. She told me earlier that she was going to take a nap. She seemed to have been exhausted by her last experience, so she's probably still asleep.

WHAT HAPPENED AT ELISE'S HOUSE

I got back from visiting with Elise about three hours ago. It's taken me this long to thoroughly examine the events, but I am now ready to relate all the details as they occurred from the moment I walked into her house.

***

I walked through the Annica Gardens to Elise's back door. The children, who were playing with Opi, the dog, confirmed my thought that their mother was taking a nap. I knocked firmly on the door, received no response, and let myself in. I decided that if she was asleep, I could pour a glass of cold water on her head—just as she had done to me that day when she found me napping under the Linden tree.

I could hear Elise singing in her bedroom, so I headed down the hallway, listening to the song. It was a new composition and I had not yet heard it. The door was open a few inches and I paused for a moment in the hall, not wanting to disturb her in case she was recording for another album.

As I listened, it became clear to me that this was not something she would include on an album that would reach the world by way of a computer download, which is her usual practice. Rather, this was some sort of cosmic communication—strange, beautiful, and haunting. I couldn't make out any recognizable language in the words she was using, and she was doing absolutely impossible things with the modulation of her voice.

I determined to wait and listen quietly in the hall, and only announce my presence when she had finished her song. Things didn't go quite as I planned.

I began to notice an odd color frequency of Purple-Blue

139

seeping through the wood of the door and the spaces around it. These color vibrations seemed to be responding to or in synchrony with her voice. At first, I thought they were coming from the Creation Frequency — that she had somehow hooked into it — but then I realized that they were not. They were more independent, like a thick band or wave, or an ocean of honey coming through her wooden door, shimmering purple in hue. The door was being consumed by the slow flood of the sweet, softly-colored goo of cosmic light.

"What on Earth is she doing?" I wondered out loud.

I put my hand to the door to push it open and became caught up in the Purple-Blue ooze. I was alarmed at first, but then I felt the bones and joints of my chest and shoulders pop and I was gently relieved of the pain that lingered from an injury to that area years before.

I also noticed that I was breathing deeper and with more ease than I have in years, as I've had to contend with asthma since birth. I've often wondered why in the world God hadn't healed me of this terrible malady. I realized in that instant that God had been saving my healing experience for this specific moment in time, perhaps so that it could be entered into the pages of *Mary's Diary* as an example meant to convey a specific message to one or more of those who will take the time to read it.

I peeked into the room. Elise was lying on her back in bed, covers pulled up to her chin, with her eyes closed. Her entire body radiated Purple-Blue, but it flowed with greatest force from her mouth and the middle of her forehead. The entire room was submerged in a deep and comforting ocean of Song-Color, welling up from within Elise's body. The energy spilled out, filled the room, and began to splash out through the bedroom walls. My body felt lighter with every step I took towards the bed, as if huge weights were being lifted from every muscle.

I assumed that she was awake, so I called her name. She did not respond, and I realized after nudging her that she was not awake at all.

Elise was emanating these energies while in a deep sleep. For a moment, I was dumbfounded. I decided to listen and to observe. I perceive life energy in a way far different from anyone else on this planet. I have a gift of seeing that is not normal by human standards, and what I saw in her Song was awesome, in the literal sense of the word. I was completely awed by what I was witnessing.

Mother H began to stream images into my mind which showed that the whole of life on this planet and then some was being enveloped by the sound Elise was creating. I recognized that the intonations and "words" were being streamed directly from our Home on Hectarus—our Heaven—and were completely separate from the Creation Frequency. Elise had become a transformer of sorts for a powerful new Hectaran frequency that Mary had described and that we had both been waiting for. Her spirit being was receiving the signal, and her body's voice was boosting and transmitting it to all of humanity. Mary had told us about the particular wave of God's healing energy that she had aligned and set in place for humanity as soon as *Volume Two* had been released to the world. Here, now, was the direct link, this ray of Elise's voice streaming it down, through, and back up. My vision allowed me to see what it was doing for the whole of life here on Earth.

I sat down cross-legged on the floor beside Elise's bed in order to take it all in. It was one of those rare times in my life that I was speechless, but two thoughts came to my mind: *all-consuming, and wonderful.* All I could do was breathe it in.

It was definitely an *in-between* moment. I knew that later I would see some dramatic news alerts on TV or receive some sort of information from Mother H or Mary or Annie about The Great Plan as a result of the alien permeation frequency that was being released by Elise. At first, I was sure that one of the Family was helping her with this, but none of the three were directly present, and none of them responded to my calls during the experience. I realized that this particular gift was Elise's alone—by way of the Will of God of course.

I have no idea how long I sat there while my spirit-being flew out of this realm, leaving behind the body I use in the mundane. The healing that was saturating this planet engulfed my own body as Elise's sounds sent me spirit-flying throughout the universe. The only other experience where I had been lifted out of this realm not by my own will was when Mary first took me back to Hectarus, as I related in *Volume 1* of *The Diary*.

What struck me as odd is that I was very much aware of being in multiple realms at once, but it was all according to the energy streaming from Elise in her room. Even though I was flying out beyond Hectarus through new nebulae I had never seen before, I was also enjoying what was happening in my own body. I could see and feel it all, but the clear vision of how this Song permeated each and every person on this planet, without their even knowing it, was truly the most spectacular thing.

I am not a very musically-oriented person, so I won't even begin to describe how it all sounded. All I can say is that it was heavenly, like Mother H, the angel that she is, was all wrapped up in each little subatomic ray of Elise's Song. Mother's rays of nurturance, nourishment, and Life were the substance of these sounds.

My presence finally did disrupt the flow of Elise's

singing, for lack of a better word. She woke up, the color vanishing at the same time.

***

Elise rubbed her eyes, and said, "Oh, hello, Din," as if nothing supernaturally strange and wonderful had happened at all.

"Hi there. Where have you been?"

"Um, hold on, I have to remember where I am now first."

"Yeah, no kidding. That's okay, take your time."

Elise sat up, looked around, and said, "It's such a disappointment to have to come back here after something like that."

"I won't take that comment personally because I know exactly what you mean," I said, feeling a bit wistful myself. "So, you are aware of what just happened?" I got up from the floor, pulled her desk chair over to the bed, and sat.

"Uh, well, yes and no," Elise said softly. "I know that I was singing, and that I was very far away. I don't really remember everything I was singing. I also know that my body was asleep, but I was also using it at the same time."

We were both shaking our heads.

"Do you realize how insane that sounds?" Elise said.

"No, not to me, it doesn't. We'll keep you away from the doctors, though. I wouldn't want to see you get locked away in a strait jacket."

"Ha, ha, Din. That's only partly funny."

"Yeah, well, that's because you have almost zero sense of humor, Miss Serious. Annie told you to lighten up, didn't she?"

Elise replied, "If I got any lighter, I wouldn't be able to stay in this body. Right now, I feel like my insides really aren't even here. Whatever sounds I was making had something to do with the fact that there has been a tremendous healing wave cascading across this whole planet."

"Tell me about it," I said encouragingly. Elise's awareness of her gifts had progressed much further than I ever imagined they would have at this point, and I was curious as to the extent of what she was really remembering about herself.

She thought for a moment before she spoke. "The work on this planet is getting streamlined, Din. God and Mother just used my voice to work something huge, and I am both joyous and concerned right now because of it."

"Huh?"

"Don't get me wrong, the frequencies of direct healing are strong right now here on Earth, but I'm deeply concerned for all the people who are on the edge of indecision or living in ignorance about The Great Plan. We're going to see things get ugly and crazy in this world because the healing that just washed through will not only cleanse deeply that which has been polluted but will assist all those requesting and ready to receive healing from above. This has been true for two millennia and now it's been quickened and intensified. I'm just very concerned about the number of people on this planet who are knowingly choosing not to awaken to a true devotion of God, as well as the ones who are still living in ignorance. Din, there are going to be major calamities in the near future because of the intensity of the dissonance caused by conflicting human emotions on this world."

***

I knew she was right, as I already had been informed by Mother H of many of those calamities about to befall mankind. Not just natural disasters—and there will be plenty—but terrible accidents, fires, terrorism, political scandals, as well as vicious, diabolical political battles for government control here in America, unlike any other time in American history. One of the major political parties will be completely taken over by evil and seek as its only cause the destruction of good in America. Christianity, morality, all that is good, will be fiercely attacked by those who will be illegally elected to positions of authority within the government. The stage has been set for these things to occur. The majority of mankind has fallen prey to the false promises of the politicians now in power all over the globe, as well as the fanatical despots who have enslaved many third-world countries.

Another smaller group of people has been lulled into a state of self-induced euphoria and false hope by the feel-good philosophies that are saturating the world culture like an invisible plague. These philosophies are among the most dangerous problems on Earth today. They are not only contributing to the distortion of the Creation Frequency, but they are diverting humanity away from the straight and narrow—the simple way that leads to the Unconditional Love of God.

It would benefit everyone to go back and reread the last few pages of *Volume I: The Strong Witch Society*, just to refresh the memory of what is to come, paying special attention to these words:

> *Treat this as fiction if you wish, but it will be a terrible thing to find out at the last moment of the last day that it was true. Very terrible.*

There are some who do not like hearing about such negative things, but that does not make that statement inaccurate. Mankind resides in a universe subject to the principle of duality. One cannot have the good without the bad. As this is the third volume of Mary's diary, it is vitally important that the grave nature of the Truth be expressed as clearly as possible, so that mankind has the opportunity to return to The One Who is The Only One who can rid this world of negativity forever, the Creator God. Humanity cannot do this by itself.

***

Elise and I sat in silence for a while before she finally said, "I feel like I just gave birth. I am tired, but ecstatic. It's similar to what my labor and deliveries were like, only this time there's a deep clarity that goes way beyond me, my babies, or my own family. Life reigns triumphant, and it's everlasting, but the knowledge that there could be millions or billions of people who will not make the correct decision makes me feel as if I had a billion miscarriages all at once."

I considered her metaphor and shifted uncomfortably in my seat. "Well, I can't say that I can empathize," I said, "but I am happy that you just said this. I believe you've reconnected with one of your most vital gifts, Elise, and since you've already been sharing your songs with the world through your albums, I think it's time that you bring these Purple Goo songs straight to the ears of humanity in real time."

"What the heck are you talking about? I think you may be the one who needs the straitjacket now, Din."

"Tell me, what did you see, while you were asleep and singing? You said you were aware of singing, but you weren't in your body at that time. What were your perceptions of the experience, and how long were you actually singing?"

At that point, her children entered the room. "Mommy started singing really soon after she laid down to take a nap," one of them said. "She told us she really needed rest, and that if we needed anything, we should go next door and bug you. We stayed outside, but we could hear her singing the whole time we were playing in the Gardens."

Shocked by the statement, I looked at Elise. "You were asleep and singing for over five hours. What, in God's name, did you see?"

The children jumped onto Elise's bed, kissed her, and then ran out of the room, slamming the door as they ran back to the Gardens.

Elise smiled and her gaze turned inward. "Well, it kept changing. I think I started singing the moment I fell asleep. I remember seeing billions of human beings, walking all over the planet. They were bustling here and there, going about their daily business. They all looked like tiny ants because I just kept flying higher and higher with the Song. The Song was moving me, but I was the one controlling the melody and the flow of my breath. At some point, I entered the Temple on Hectarus. I went into the room with the giant Orange-Pink stone. I swam into the stone and stayed there awhile. That's when the Song started to change. It began to take me over completely, and I gave in entirely because it felt so rich, so completely delicious.

"When I was finished inside the stone, I saw myself within a powerful jet of White light, only it was more than White. It was an entire symphony of Color, and my voice became the lead instrument. The Spirit of God was the conductor, for sure, and I was aware of my breath and how I breathed in relation to the sound.

"Then I saw myself shooting back to Earth, seeing all those billions of people again, only this time the Song was hitting the planet faster than light. I was careening in and out of the Earth, following a pattern like a Möbius strip. Yes, this is exactly the way the Song of myself was flying through the whole of this little planet. It was so intense and so wonderful. I could see and feel the organic nature of the Earth and all its peoples, but I was also experiencing its true nature. I was resonating inside the spirit reality of life on Earth, and the Song was helping to make that reality stronger for the minds of people down here."

"Amazing. Go on," I said.

"It was joyful, and the excitement grew within me. I kept asking for more of this life Song to strengthen through myself. I sensed how the activity was actually affecting all of life everywhere, not just in this universe, and then ... I remembered everything, Din."

"Everything? You remember it all now?" I could barely contain my excitement.

"Yes, Din, I know now exactly who I am, and many memories have returned. But I won't speak of it right now. This is most important."

"You are absolutely correct, and this is as it should be, Elise. I was about to say you need your rest, but the opposite is true, I guess. The kids are probably out there eating grass, so I think you guys should make some dinner. Just come back to the three-dimensional realm now, and don't go flying off again for a while, alright?"

"Alright." Elise smiled and exhaled very deeply.

I left Elise's house and sent the children back in. As I walked through the Garden, I heard the unusual sound of both a mourning dove and a mockingbird, filling the air with the combination of their two widely different songs, the first with its soothing descending call, and the latter with its unpredictable song of fanciful flight. I had never heard these two perform at the same time before. It was as if they were composing a duet, sharing the melody together. It was lovely.

"We have to be prepared for the unexpected now, Mother, don't we?" I said, pointing my face upward into the beautiful blue sky.

I latched the Garden gate behind me and returned to the other house. I didn't really expect Mother H to answer my question, but I knew she was there. I could feel her smiling down at me.

An Urgent Command from Annie

It is only fitting that at least one entry in this Volume of Mary's Diary should be written while I am seated under the Linden Tree in the midst of the Annica Gardens. It was not long ago that I first began writing Mary's thoughts down on paper in longhand here in the shade of this sweet and faithful friend.

I've had many magical experiences under this Linden—some quite dramatic, and others so subtle that I was unaware of the event until Annie or Mother H reminded me of the circumstances. I'm kind of hoping as I lay back in my lounge chair this morning, soaking up the bright sunshine of early April, that Mother H might just pop in on me and do something a little bit wild. Compared to last week with the dramatic experience in Elise's bedroom, this week has been pretty mundane.

Since the awakening of our latest Strong Weet, Christa, very little has happened of a supernatural nature aside from Elise's experience. Maybe that's a good thing. There are good supernatural experiences and there are bad supernatural experiences, and a person can't always pick and choose which one is going to be the flavor of the day. Even I tend to forget that not all of the seemingly magical moments come from Mother H or Annie. Some are brought on by dark forces that are in opposition to what we are attempting to do here on Earth. That's the unfortunate thing about living in a universe partially controlled by the Principles of Polarity and Duality. Regardless of what some would have humanity believe, the only Being capable of amending these great Principles is God, and God has only amended the Laws three times throughout all of Earth's history, going back to the seeding of Annica three-and-a-half million years ago.

Magical moments? Those are from God as well, and they only happen when necessary. So I doubt seriously that one of those is going to …

Father?

Annie! Talk about a magical moment.

Father, you know as well as I do that you are perfectly capable of creating your own magical moments now, any time you wish. You also know that magic has nothing to do with it. There is no such thing as magic. Occurrences that are mistaken for magic on this world are really the miraculous workings of God in times when there is need of such things as miracles. Mother explained that in the VOLUME ONE *of* THE DIARY.

I know. But you are still my daughter, and every time you pop in on me, I count that as a miracle.

That's very sweet. I love you too. At this moment, though, there is something that you must do, and you must do it quickly. Much depends upon it.

Okay. I hope it's something I can do under this tree. It's such a beautiful day.

I'll fill you in, Father, but I'm afraid you are going to have to leave blessed Linden for a while and take a little drive. You have a meeting to attend.

I do?

You need to drive to St. Louis, where you will visit a place called The Old Mill. You're meeting is in three hours and they will be expecting you.

They will? Who the heck are they? And what the heck is The Old Mill?

The Old Mill is an adult care facility, and 'they' are the manager and a few members of her staff.

You mean a rest home?

I do. Grandma will reveal more to you as you speak with the manager and her staff. All you will need to do is be yourself. Elise will be going with you.

What, I need a chaperon?

You do not. It is for Elise's own sake that she is going along.

Okay, this sounds intriguing.

It's more than that. It's one of the most important things you will do while you are in this body, and it is absolutely necessary for the success of The Great Plan.

Just how important can it be? A rest home?

So important that God will be with you all the way through the experience.

That's important.

You and Elise must get used to that. You are being prepared for something that is of greatest importance in the Eyes of God. It will soon be time to reveal to this world a new experience. Do you remember Phase Two?

Are you referring to what I think you're referring to?

I am indeed.

I was wondering when God would get around to that. I believe it has been almost three hundred years since God unleashed—

Enough, Father. Concentrate on the task at hand. If you leave right now you will be on time for your appointment.

I suppose that's a good idea, huh?

It is. Now go.

But who—

You will ask for the manager, Mrs. Carter. Samantha Carter.

You're kidding.

I am not kidding.

As in, Major Samantha Carter? Amanda Tapping, SG-1, Major Carter. The woman of my dreams?

It's strictly a coincidence. No relation.

That's a relief. I think.

Although there is a slight resemblance.

Stop it.

Can't you take a joke?

But what in the world am I supposed to say to her? How does she even know who I am?

She has read Mother's Diary.

Both volumes?

Both. And she wants to meet you.

How did she set up an appointment with me?

She sent you an email.

I don't recall getting her email.

You didn't, Father. I intercepted it and made all of the arrangements for you.

What, you didn't trust me to do it?

I was following Grandma's wishes.

Oh, that.

Grandma didn't want you to have any preconceived images or attitudes in your mind when you visited the Old Mill. You know how you can be.

Come on, Annie. I wouldn't do anything drastic at an old folk's home.

I know that, Father. That's not what Grandma was concerned about. She wishes for both you and Elise to be totally relaxed and completely centered on what you will experience there. After your meeting with Mrs. Carter, you will understand everything.

I just hope I don't slip up and call her Sam.

***

What Happened at the Old Mill Care Home

Elise and I were met at the front entrance of The Old Mill by an attendant who had to push a button in order to release the security lock on the massive, double-paned, glass doors in order to allow our entrance.

"Wow," I whispered to Elise as we entered the building. "I wonder why all the security?"

"Use your head, Din," Elise said. "What part of *care facility* don't you understand?"

"I get it. They're afraid the old folks will escape out the front."

"It's been known to happen."

The attendant had us sign in at a station near the entrance, and then led us down a hallway toward a group of five offices arranged in a circle around a large and luxurious waiting room.

"This is lovely," Elise said. "Look at the floor. Is that marble?"

"Probably some sort of manufactured flooring that just looks like marble."

"I don't know. It looks like the real thing to me. It must cost a pretty penny to move your grandpa into a place like this."

The attendant invited us to take a seat on one of the large over-stuffed couches in the reception area, then disappeared into what appeared to be the largest of the offices in the circle.

Moments later, both the attendant and a woman I presumed to be Mrs. Carter exited the office and walked briskly over to greet us.

"It is such an honor to meet you." Mrs. Carter extended

her hand to both Elsie and me.

"Thank you so much," Elise said with a smile.

"My privilege," I said as I shook her hand.

"Please, let's go into my office where we can be comfortable."

Her office was furnished pleasantly and simply with a glass-top desk, a couple of leather chairs, and a few potted plants. There was a large bookcase near her desk and a single, cheerful painting of a large vase with pink and yellow flowers hung on the opposite wall. The nicest part was the large window behind her desk. It practically filled that entire end of the room and overlooked one of the most beautiful gardens I have ever seen on this world, rivaling even the famous Missouri Botanical Garden just a few blocks down from The Old Mill.

Mrs. Carter motioned for us to sit in the leather chairs while she seated herself behind her desk.

"Forgive me for repeating myself, but it is so wonderful to meet you both. I've read your books and I just can't tell you how they have affected me."

"They seem to affect everyone who reads them, Mrs. Carter," I said.

"Please, call me Sam. We aren't very formal around here."

"Sam," I stuttered. Elise stifled a laugh.

"Well, Sam." I said. "I must admit that it is kind of unusual for us to be invited—"

"To a care facility?" she finished.

"Well, yeah."

"What he means, Sam," Elise said, taking the lead, "is that we get all kinds of invites for meetings and the like, but I believe this is the first time we've ever been to an establishment such as this."

"I'm afraid my inviting you here has two purposes."

I could tell Sam was fishing around in her head for the right words.

"The first is entirely selfish, I'm afraid—I just wanted to meet you both. I lead a small reading group here in St. Louis. Well, not too small really. There are about twenty of us, mostly folks who had already read one or both of the books and just kind of gravitated into the group. For the past several months we have been reading and discussing both volumes." She smiled.

"Well then," Elise said cheerfully. "It's Din and I who should be honored to meet you, Sam. How very kind of you to choose our books for your group."

"Everyone in the group agrees that they are the most unusual books any of us have ever read, and I have to tell you that we all believe that what you two and Mary have written in the *Diary* is one hundred percent true."

"Interesting," I said. "I mean, it really is interesting because it's unusual for us to hear that an entire reading group believes everything in the books. We're used to a rather mixed critique from groups we've met with before."

"Din's right about that," Elise said. "Most of the groups have chosen the books for purposes of what I call hobby discussion or, in the case of colleges and universities, for purely analytical or critical reasons."

"Teaching their students how not to write," I said. "I'm just kidding, of course."

"Of course you are," Sam replied. "The books are very well done."

"But you said there were two reasons why you asked us here today, Sam," Elise reminded her.

"I did." Sam's expression grew serious. "And it is precisely because my entire group believes so strongly in what you have written that we all agreed we should invite you here."

I looked at her quizzically.

"You see," Sam continued, "we have some very … umm … interesting … residents here at The Old Mill, and since nearly everyone in the reading group is related to at least one of them, we all felt that you two would be interested in a tour of the facility."

"Okay," I said slowly.

"I've confused you, haven't I?"

"Well, a bit," I replied.

"It isn't so much the facility that I want you to see. It's one of the residents."

"You mean one of the older folk who live here?" Elise asked.

"This one isn't quite so old, but yes, she does live here."

"Okay," I said again and looked at Elise.

"Why don't you both come with me," Sam said as she rose from her chair and walked toward the door. "I hope I'm doing the right thing here. I just have a feeling that you need to meet this resident."

Elise and I got up and followed Sam. She led us on a brief tour of The Old Mill, which turned out to be much larger on the inside than it had appeared from the outside. We wound up at the end of a long hallway at the back of the facility, in front of a pair of large, heavy-looking oak doors. The sign hung over the doors declared them to be the entrance to the Alzheimer's Unit.

I was seriously beginning to wonder what we were doing there when I heard the voice. *Just go with flow, Father.*

"Okay, Annie. It's your show," I muttered.

"I beg your pardon?" Sam looked at me.

"Oh, nothing. Just thinking aloud." I knew I'd better stop doing that or she might think I needed to move in to The Old Mill.

Sam pushed a button on the wall beside the door. "This

rings for the attendant inside," she explained.

The attendant, a large woman with arms like a wrestler's, opened the door and guided us down another hallway to a lovely sitting room occupied by about a dozen elderly residents, each one engaged in some sort of solitary activity, apparently oblivious to the world around them.

There was a large flat-screen TV hanging on one wall. It was turned on and a few of the residents were facing it, but only one appeared to be actually watching it. It was airing a black-and-white movie that looked like it was filmed back in the forties. I realized it was Meet Me in St. Louis, starring Judy Garland. How appropriate.

Sam called this room the parlor, and it did resemble an old-fashioned Victorian parlor. The sofas and chairs were all styled in the fashion of that era, and the paintings were as well. There was even one of those old-fashioned phonographs—the kind that need to be wound by hand in order to play—standing in a corner. It had an old record on it that looked as if it might have been played a lot.

And there was that lovely garden again. A large picture window behind one of the red velvet sofas displayed a scene that could have been taken from our Annica Gardens. Dozens of varieties of flowers in every color imaginable were already popping out in the early spring sunshine. Red brick pathways wove in and out and around the flower beds. There were Roman-styled statues placed here and there, at least three large water fountains, and Victorian-style black iron benches were placed conveniently throughout the garden so that one did not have to walk far in order to find a seat from which to admire the view.

"Your garden is stunning," I said.

"It truly is," Sam said. "Would you like to go out and have a walk?"

"I would love it. Elise?"

"Oh yes," she said. "It's amazing how it reminds me of Annica, only smaller, of course."

Sam turned to Elise and said pointedly, "That's exactly what I thought when I read your descriptions of the Annica Gardens in the books."

"Elise is right," I said. "I'd swear you read the books before planting the garden, but I can see that isn't possible. I think that garden out there predates the publication of our books by at least a year or two."

"By about five years," Sam said. "And to be honest, I had nothing to do with it. I've only been here for five years. This garden has been under the care of one person since it was planted. I'll fill you in as we walk."

"I wish Sit were with us. She'd love to see this," I said.

"Perhaps all of your Strong Weet will make a visit here one day soon." Sam grinned as she led us out into the beautiful garden.

The first thing that caught my eye was a small sign affixed to a post next to the garden's main entrance. Elise and I both saw the sign at exactly the same moment, and we had to stop to get our breath. The sign read, "ANNIE'S GARDEN."

I stood transfixed and I heard the sharp intake of breath from Elise that told me she was as surprised as I.

"You've just noticed the sign," Sam said. "It was not placed there by me nor by any other member of the reading group. It was handmade and placed there the day this garden was begun over nine years ago by the person who planted the very first flower, and who has overseen this garden ever since."

"Okay." That was all I could say.

Elise spoke without moving her gaze from the little sign. "I'm not sure where this is all headed, Sam, but I'm enjoying the ride so far."

I turned to Sam and looked hard and long into her eyes. "Are you suggesting that the Annie named on the sign is our Annie?"

"I'll let you be the judge of that," Sam said softly. "I've taken the liberty of sending an attendant for the resident who is responsible for both this garden, and the sign at its entrance."

"Resident?" Elise and I exclaimed simultaneously.

"You heard me correctly." Sam chose her next words carefully. "And when you meet her, I believe you will understand why I, and all of the readers' group, thought it would be prudent for me to invite you here today."

Another attendant, not so large as the first, approached us from the main building accompanied by a delicate, petite woman. The little woman had linked her arm through the attendant's, and the attendant held her hand in a way that not only gave the woman stability, but conveyed affection as well. The woman, who was older but not yet elderly, looked directly into my eyes and smiled one of the sweetest, prettiest smiles I had ever experienced.

I looked at Elise, who was smiling her wide inviting smile. Sam, too, looked as if she were about to burst with joy at seeing this little lady coming toward us. Even the attendant was grinning ear to ear. And, I swear, flowers still in bud opened wide as she came near them, turning their petals toward the pretty turquoise sky.

I have to admit that even I—being who I am, and given what I have seen in my life—was enchanted by the delightful scene that was being played out here at The Old Mill. God had indeed brought us here for a reason, and I could feel the Presence of God very strongly now.

The little woman resident came right up to us and, with a happy little laugh, shook our hands with great vigor.

"I'm so delighted to meet both of you," she said sincerely. "I'm Melody, and I'm from the stars."

Sam looked at Elise and me. I could tell she was trying to judge our reactions to the statement that Melody had just made, but given everything that was unfolding before us with such purpose, neither Elise nor I, were even slightly surprised by what she'd just said.

"We were just admiring your garden," Elise said, beaming her smile at Melody.

"Oh, my dear, it is not my garden," came the reply. "I had nothing to do with this wonderful place. It is all the work of God. I believe I dug the first hole many years ago, but that was all I ever did. Haven't touched it since."

I turned to Sam, a question in my eyes.

"She's telling you the truth. Really," Sam affirmed. "No one actually sees her tending the garden. There is an attendant present every moment she's out here, but the attendant says that all she does is sit in the middle of the garden and sing."

Tears began to form in Elise's eyes.

"I'm not in charge of gardens where I come from," Melody said. "You know that. There is another who fills that duty."

I turned to Sam, "Are you telling us that no one else tends this garden? It's never been weeded? The flowers have never been pinched or pruned? Insects have never been tended to?"

"We have on staff professional gardeners who take very good care of the yards and garden areas surrounding the outside of this complex, but not one living soul has ever touched Annie's Garden. What's more, it's never been watered. Look around—there are no hoses, water cans, or even water faucets."

"God waters here." Melody made a sweeping gesture

with her arms as she looked around at the flowers. "I am not a gardener. That is not my gift. That gift belongs to our dear friend. You know that."

"Do you have a special gift, Melody?" I asked her, feeling an uncontrollable surge of love welling up within me.

"Oh, I certainly do, dear." Melody's eyes glistened with tears as she said, "My gift is compassion."

She said the last word, compassion, with such softness that Elise could no longer contain her emotions, and even Sam was crying.

"You have compassion for these flowers?"

"I have compassion for all of God's creations. That is my job in this life," Melody pronounced matter-of-factly.

I was getting teary eyed, as well. I turned toward Sam and said, "Can we talk to you over there for just a minute?" I pointed to a little alcove off to the left.

"Of course," Sam replied. "Melody, you wait here with Shirley. We won't be long."

"Oh, you take as long as you would like, Sam. Shirley is my dear friend and I love being with her." Shirley, too, was in tears.

Elise, Sam, and I stepped into the shelter of the alcove. It was a few moments before any of us could speak.

"Okay, Sam," I whispered. "You gotta fill us in a little here. What's Melody's story? What's she doing in here? She looks like she's only about forty, but I can tell by her conversation that her mind is a little bit different from most folks her age."

"Melody may look much younger, but she will be sixty-two this coming July. She has been diagnosed as having both dementia and Alzheimer's disease."

I looked down at my feet.

"She doesn't seem to be the violent sort," Elise said.

"Not all Alzheimer's patients are violent. But that wasn't

the diagnosis that got her admitted to The Old Mill."

"Oh?" I asked.

"It was her conversation with her doctor that did it," Sam said.

"Can you tell us, or is it confidential?" Elise asked.

"Melody began showing signs of Alzheimer's disease about three months before she came here. She was taken to her doctor several times during that period. She seemed quite healthy and able to converse, but it was what she said to the doctor during those conversations that made him think she needed our care."

"I'm all ears," I said.

"You are going to find this quite interesting." Sam grinned as she looked back at Melody, who smiled and waved her hand in return. "I'll try to sum this up as briefly as possible. First of all, be aware that Melody has never read your books, nor has anyone ever discussed them with her. The first interactions with her doctor included a question and answer session — simple things that doctors ask all folks who are suspected of having the disease like What year is this? Who is the president of the USA? Can you remember when you were born?

"Melody got the first two answers right, but it was all downhill after that. She told the doctor that she was born on another planet that was located about four hundred and fifty light years from Earth. She couldn't remember the name of the planet, but she insisted that she had been born there thousands of years ago, and that all of her family and friends were waiting for her to come back home.

"The doctor then asked her if she could tell him about her family "back home." The doctor told me how Melody responded and her answers sounded like they came right out of the pages of *Mary's Diary*.

"She said that several of her family members now residing on her home planet had been jumping about willy-nilly all over this planet for many years, but this is the last time. They won't ever have to come back here again because everything is wrapping up. She also told the doctor that she was one of the last of her family remaining "down here", and that she still had a job to do before she could go back home and join those who had already returned."

"Compassion," I said.

"Compassion. After the reading group finished reading both volumes of *Mary's Diary*, I had Melody's doctor come in and visit with us. He was reluctant to admit anything at the time, but we gave him copies of the books. He read them, and afterward, even though he wouldn't publicly admit it, I could tell he was convinced that Melody might not be as diseased as everyone believed her to be."

"If what you tell us is the truth," I said to Sam, "then this garden is indeed a miracle, and Melody is most likely one of us."

"Can you not feel the Presence of God in this place?" Sam said earnestly. "Sometimes, when I am very tired, or just emotionally drained from being with some of the residents, I come out here and sit on the bench right in the middle of the garden, the one Melody always sits on. I sit and I begin to weep. I'm at my lowest. I'm beat to the roots. But from out of nowhere, every time, a warm and gentle breeze brushes against my face. It can be the middle of winter and this warm, soft wind touches my face and I feel the Presence of something so big, so wonderful, that all I can do is raise my hands up to the heavens and smile. And sometimes when this happens to me, I look around and here comes Melody from out of nowhere, with her big smile on her face, her hands clasped to her bosom, to sit down beside me. She doesn't say a word. She doesn't have to."

"God is present now, Sam." Elise says softly. "God is with us here."

"Just as Annie promised me," I said softly. "Annie told me God would be here supervising this entire visit. All we had to do was be ourselves and we would understand."

"She is a Strong Weet, Din," Elise said.

"Indeed, she is."

"I can't believe I am so blessed as to be present for this," Sam whispered. "I am so honored."

"God does not wish for feelings of honor," Elise told Sam. "God wishes only that you know this is all Truth, and that you will from this day forward devote your life to The Great Plan of God."

"I will," Sam said softly. "Believe me. How can anyone remain the same after being given such a wealth of experience as this?"

"Now what?" I asked Elise.

"I'm not really sure."

At that moment another attendant walked up to us, pushing one of the other residents in a wheel chair, and spoke to Sam.

"Mrs. Carter, I hate to bother you, but Dr. Meredith has called and she's going to be an hour late today."

"Oh shoot, I have that technicians meeting to go to." Sam said. "That's okay though, I can be late for that. Thanks Debbie."

"And who is this lovely lady?" Elise stepped over to the resident in the wheelchair.

The attendant smiled and said, "This is Mrs. Taylor."

"Mrs. Taylor has been with us for about three years," explained Sam. "She was just like she is now when we admitted her. She's never spoken a word while she has been here. Never opens her eyes. Never leaves that chair except for when the attendants lift her into her bed at night."

Elise, tearing up again, bent down toward Mrs. Taylor. She placed her hand on the aged resident's head and said very softly, "Blessed God, heal this one, for in her condition she is not capable of having faith. Please heal this one."

I placed my hand on Mrs. Taylor's shoulder and spoke the same words, "Please heal this one."

Mrs. Taylor began to slowly raise her head. Her movement startled the attendant, who stepped to the side and raised her hands to her chin.

"Mrs. Taylor?" Sam spoke loudly. "Mrs. Taylor?"

Mrs. Taylor lifted her head all the way up, slowly opened her eyes, and spoke the first word she had spoken in years. "Hello."

I could tell Sam was afraid to move, but she said firmly, "Debbie, you go call Dr. Meredith back and tell her to get out here right now."

Then, walking over to Mrs. Taylor, and taking her right hand into both of hers, Sam said, "Mrs. Taylor. My name is Sam. Do you know where you are?"

"I'm right here," was her weak reply. "I am with Angels."

"Merciful heaven," Sam said. "This is incredible."

"It's just another miracle, Sam." I smiled.

Suddenly, Melody, her voice joyful and strong, called out, "That's it! Her name is Sit — our friend, the Master Gardener from back home. You know her, Elise. She's your sister."

BACK IN THE ANNICA GARDENS

Elise and I stayed at The Old Mill until Dr. Meredith arrived. She had been anxious to see for herself that Mrs. Taylor was not only upright and awake in her wheelchair, but that she was speaking full sentences. Once, when no one was paying attention, she'd even gotten out of the wheelchair and headed off deeper into the garden before Debbie was able to bring her back to her chair.

The doctor had, of course, been unable to explain anything that had occurred. She was quite familiar with Mrs. Taylor's background and condition and was totally baffled by what she found when she arrived. All she could do was shake her head in wonderment at the apparent miracle. Dr. Meredith took a moment to look around at the garden before going inside with Mrs. Taylor to examine her more thoroughly. "What's with this place?" she asked. "I've never seen anything like it."

While the others were going back inside, Elise and I took the opportunity to slip away. Before we left, though, I pulled Sam aside and said to her, "I'm sure we will be seeing more of you and Melody as time goes forward."

Sam held my hand tightly. "Must you go right now?" she asked. "Please, do come back soon."

"We won't leave you, Sam," I told her. "I must admit, I didn't see any of this coming, but the events of this visit have shown me that you and Melody are an essential part of our little family down here. I promise you, we will see each other again."

***

So, here I am, back under the Linden tree. Elise and Sit are strolling around the Annica Gardens together. Elise is telling Sit about our visit to The Old Mill, while I ponder it all, wondering what the next steps should be.

I wave my hand at the others and shout out to them, "Hey, you two! Come over and have a seat. We need to have a powwow."

"She knew my name?" Sit asks as she settles into a lounge chair near my own. "This Melody?"

"She did," I confirm.

"Then there's no doubt that she's one of us. But isn't this going to be a bit awkward? Melody has Alzheimer's and she's living in a care home over a hundred miles away. How can she take part in our work, while she's so separated from us?

"Her gift of compassion knows no distance," Elise replies.

"Annie told me we'd find a Strong Weet at The Old Mill. I thought at first that it might be Sam, even though her Glow didn't seem quite right for someone of that level," I confessed. "I was beginning to think there was something wrong with me when I was unable to merge my Glow with hers."

"I thought that as well." Elise said. "Melody surprised me. She sure knew who you were, Sit, and she knew that you are my true sister."

"Wow. Okay, she might have Alzheimer's by medical standards, but it sure sounds to me like she's fully Awakened," Sit said.

I looked from one to the other of them. "Since when have you two known that you are sisters from Hectarus?"

They looked at each other and laughed. "Longer than you realized, apparently," Elise said.

"Okay, that's wonderful. I was waiting for this

relationship to be revealed, but apparently the moment has come and gone." I was actually quite amazed that these two Strong Weet had been privately discussing things I thought only I was aware of.

"Now all we have to do is figure out what to do about Melody," I said. "Where is that daughter of mine when I need her? So, Annie, wherever you are, what are we going to do with a Strong Weet who has Alzheimer's and who is locked away in an old folks home a hundred and twenty miles from here? And will you please appear so we can see you while we visit?"

In a flash — literally—Annie appeared before us as a translucent golden Glow, similar to the way she has appeared during the Gatherings. This form of manifestation is primarily an electrical imaging technique used by Annie and Mother H that involves enlarging a tiny portion of their Glow into an image. This is not to be confused with a common holographic projection. A hologram has no substance and very little energy. A person can run their hand through one and nothing would happen. The images produced by Annie and Mother are quite different. They are pure electric energy vibrating at a frequency of such intensity that it is undetectable by human measurement. If one were to run a hand through one of these images, that hand would be vaporized in an instant.

Elise and Sit can see this image of Annie as she hovers about three feet off the ground above the buried Annican Altar at the center of Annica Gardens. Annie has appeared before them in this form several times. They're getting used to it, but they are still a bit cautious and keep their distance, as they know that without their ninth strand of DNA they cannot afford to get too close to her vibratory essence. Until the vibrations of their own Spirit Beings are retuned internally, their human physiology would also be in danger of being harmed by her Glow. It's always fun for me to watch their faces when Annie appears. They reflect the excitement of a couple of kids at Christmas, tempered with a little bit of caution. Although they are both aware of the incredible power contained within the small frame that Annie chooses to adopt when taking this form, neither Sit nor Elise are ever afraid in her presence. What boggles my mind the most is how Annie is indeed able to contain her energy like that. I have seen her grow in size to where her energy body stretched over millions of light years into the vastness of deep space. I have also seen her obliterate entire galaxies in a split second with a mere wave of her hand, yet here she is, looking like a teen-aged girl standing in a pretty flower garden. The obvious difference, of course, is that she is Glowing—and we can see through her.

I will keep a distance from all of you.

"I wish you didn't have to do that," Elise says. "You look so cute, I just want to hold you in my arms and cuddle you close to me."

I wish the same, Elise.

Annie's reply sounds a bit sad to me. I know many things about Annie that Elise and Sit do not yet know. One of those things is that no matter how incredibly powerful this wonderful being is, her spirit and soul are not much different from our own. I know that she longs to be with her True Family, permanently. I am fortunate that my physiology has been strengthened so that I am able to hold my daughter close to me without the fear of being destroyed in the process.

One day, Elise, you will be able to hold me, but there is much work to be done before that can happen.

"A big part of that work has to do with the instruction of the Strong Weet, and one of those is in that rest home over in St. Louis," I remind Annie. "Do you have any ideas as to how we can accomplish that?"

It will not be difficult, Father. Don't forget, there is much that Mother and I can do from where we reside that you cannot. We are already working on it.

"Well, I need to schedule another Gathering soon so we can have all the Strong Weet together in one place. It's time for us to begin Phase Two of our work down here, and we'll need everyone we have Awakened in order to do that work."

"And there are still two more out there somewhere," Sit added. "But I have faith that they will pop up soon. I am constantly amazed at how everyday circumstances bring these folks into our midst."

"Yes," Elise agreed. "I thought they'd be living all over the world and we'd have to travel around looking for them, and then fly them back here for the Gatherings."

Some of them were living in different countries up until just a few years ago. Mother and I have seen to it that they have all been able to immigrate to America in order to Awaken here at the proper moment. Time is slipping away, and it was needful to get them into the fold as quickly as possible.

"I know that Merta came here from Mexico, and I am assuming Christa was probably living in Italy at one time, but what about the new Weet, Melody?

"Melody is from Scotland," I told them. "She grew up in a village called Laggan, up in the Highlands of Scotland. She still has a cute little accent, although it isn't as pronounced as some I've heard from that region."

"Isn't that where some of your ancestors are from, Din?" Elise asks. "I've heard you talk about your Scots roots before."

"Yep. Laggan is the origin of part of my bloodline in

this physical life. I still have a few cousins over there who spend their days sitting by the loch fishing for salmon."

"I remember you mentioned Scotland in one of the books, and the important part it played in the history of this world." Sit said.

"Yes, I did. You might recall that although Annica was our main focus of development, we also seeded a group of beings in the region now known as Scotland. The old Scots ancestry stories are filled with little hints about the mysterious people who came from far away to begin the society that provided the origins for much of the culture, tradition, and heritage found throughout Scotland, Ireland, Wales and England."

One day, archaeologists will uncover proof of a civilization in Scotland, near Laggan, that is so old that it will cause them to completely rethink how they have studied their science for all of these years.

"That's gonna be fun," I said.

"When do you think that will happen?" Sit asked.

"I believe that it will coincide with the same discovery over here on Annica. And Annie is right, when these civilizations are uncovered, their discovery will rewrite human history and cause a lot of belief systems to collapse."

"Won't that be a problem for mankind?" Sit asked. "Won't that cause a little bit of turmoil around here?"

It will, but by then all choices will have been made and all decisions will be final.

"What do you mean, Annie?" Elise asked.

We will be well into the final years of The Great Plan by then. Humanity will have made the decision as to either save their world, or watch it be destroyed by the results of their own bad decisions. If they choose correctly, then, when the archaeologists discover our ancient work, we will share with them all of the marvels of those civilizations. Earth will become once again the Jewel of this universe. God will be quite pleased, and miracles will be wrought, moving every creature upon this world to give glory to their Creator once again.

"Which brings me back to my original question, dear Daughter. We have one Weet in St. Louis and two more still unaware of who they are. Don't you think that it might be time for us to use our abilities and do a little coaxing, or pull a few strings, in order to bring them all together and get them here to Annica?"

Father, I already told you that Mother and I are already pulling strings concerning Melody's situation. In fact, it should be resolved very shortly.

"What about the other two Strong Weet?" I asked.

There will be another of the Strong Weet passing through this area very soon and she will Awaken then. But there is that one other. That one is being saved until last for a very specific purpose. She will be Awakened, but not until the time is exactly right for that to occur.

"She must be some *Strong* Weet," Sit commented.

She brings her own unique strengths to the Gathering, as do you all, but her Awakening must be done when the time is right. Every Weet, including the Secondary Weet located all over this globe, are unique individuals with specific gifts. At this time, each one is being given a specific frequency and resonance and their development is being carefully guided, so that when their gifts are joined together into one, each gift will not just be added one to the other, but infinitely multiplied, resulting in unimaginable power.

ELISE MEETS THE FIFTH STRONG WEET

One of the more frustrating things about being in a physical human body is the limitation on speed. My spirit knows how to move faster than the speed of light, but unfortunately, my flesh cannot.

When I am not able to ride my horse, swim like an otter in the rushing current of a river, or sprint along a mountain trail, I can somewhat assuage my need by driving my car. Angela—Spanish pronunciation, not English—is a 1998 Honda Accord and she possesses the spirit of my horse, Blanca. Yes, I know that sounds crazy, but it's true. Angela is a man-made machine with the spirit of a horse. Even spirit-being animals have the ability to drop down into other bodies and forms.

I learned at a very early age that speed was a good way to handle the frustrations of the disturbing circumstances of my childhood. My spirit mind knew that I didn't really belong to most of the people in the family I was born to. Before I was ten years old, I was able to visualize myself shooting up and away in a burst of volcanic light, far out of the solar system—it was the easiest way to save myself from the outbursts of uncontrolled anger displayed by some of the adults in my life at the time.

I didn't just imagine it, I actually was catapulted out of this world and beyond the solar system. I knew how to do it, and I was aware in my own mind that I really was traveling wherever it was that I found myself at any given moment of the journey. I also knew however, that I couldn't be among crystal-pink nebulae and swirling vortices of starry masses all the time. Physical speed was the next best thing.

I did everything fast—running, bike riding, swimming, tree climbing, even reading. My guiding principle was that if I can't do it fast, then I am probably not interested — to be honest, it still is. And yet, my favorite animal was the turtle. I guess I needed the balance.

Here I am, twenty-five years later, reflecting on my latest speed-racer journey. It was totally unexpected, of course, but I have come to accept that the only thing I can expect is the doing of God's Will, for that is the one thing I have given the whole of my life to.

I'm just glad I didn't run into her. Din would've had my hide for hitting the car of another Strong Weet, or God forbid, causing harm to the Weet herself.

It was a crisp Saturday morning, and my kids had just gone to spend a little two-on-two time with my Earth mom and stepfather, who had driven in from St. Louis. My parents insisted that they take the children alone, telling me that I never make time for myself, and that when I do, I fill it by doing chores.

As they drove away, I grabbed the car keys, threw on my coat, hat, and scarf, and headed to the garage. I was experiencing another burning desire to move fast. The sudden gift of being offered a chance to do whatever I wanted, all by my lonesome, was a tad bit thrilling.

I took off down the country lane, and I was moving along just fine until I started to sneeze uncontrollably, seven in a row to be exact. As usual, after the sneezing fit, my nose started to itch like crazy.

"Aw, come on. I can't drive like this. I know you're here, Mary, and I'm listening, but please cut it out. I'm trying to have a little fun. Give me a break."

You do nothing without purpose, Elise. Speed will deny you the riches. Do not pass by one who possesses it strongly. It may come upon you quicker than you realize. Be careful, and be aware.

"Yup, got it. I will admire all the spirit beings as I drive past them. I will smell all the roses as I zoom along the way, I promise. But if you want to give me some clues about those riches you speak of, I'm all ears."

Just drive safely, Elise. And pay attention!

"Okay, I'm out."

After pulling out of the little country lane that leads away from the Annica land and onto a stretch of county highway lined on both sides with forest, I pushed the gas pedal down. The trees looked so thin without their leaves, but they were lovely in their sparkling icy coats of early winter frost. I could hear them call out their sweet hellos as I sped by.

I paid attention to Mary's admonition and made sure to take stock of my surroundings, watching out for other drivers or four-leggeds, but there didn't appear to be anyone out on the road as it was still early. I had decided to commit to ending up at Joey's Gelateria, my favorite ice cream parlor, but I was beginning to feel that familiar old fire—regardless of what Mary had asked me to do.

I needed to go fast. I knew that when Mary said to pay attention, it usually meant that I was going to be shown something or receive something. The excitement of not knowing what that was made my foot even heavier on the pedal. This was not a speeding expedition motivated by frustration or fear. It was just pure joy.

"We will make it a safe, speeding expedition," I said to Angela. "Mother H would cut off my head if I killed myself in a car accident." The thought made me laugh as I put on the brake to sneeze again. "Then I'd have to grow a new one."

It had snowed the previous week, and the trees still wore their glistening white coats. They held their positions like dancers in the spotlight of the sun, bowing to each other gracefully. Part of me wanted to linger to admire them, but I put my foot down again and they became a blur as my speed increased. My thoughts drifted to my exquisite, snow-colored horse, Blanca and I began to Hum. The white radiance of the spirit horse in my mind merged with the white radiance of the physical machine in which I was carried. I could only imagine what a spectacle it made for those looking down on us as the radiance interacted with the flurried landscape of blinding snow and the dancing trees. I felt my own breath turn White as well, as pure and joyous as the entire untouched ocean of layered crystal snow surrounding me.

I spoke through my Hum, "God, life is so rich with goodness."

Something from my childhood came upon me in that moment. Whenever I was in the middle of something that was potentially physically dangerous, I would hear my daddy singing a song. It was sort of a combination spiritual radar and shield, a gentle warning to alert me to the ignorance of my behavior and the need to change it, while at the same time protecting me from the worst consequences.

The song, "Softly and Tenderly Jesus is Calling," was one he'd loved, but I hadn't sung it in more than twenty years. The melody is lilting and comforting, and the sensation produced by the combination of color, melody, and the purity of the setting was blissful.

I slammed on my brakes. "God help me!"

I had just missed a woman who had jumped into my path. There was a car parked beside the road and she had been on the other side of it, hidden from view. My efforts to avoid her had resulted in a skid that left Angela with her rear tires on the pavement and her nose lodged in a snow-filled ditch. I unbuckled my seatbelt, climbed out of the car, and ran over to the woman.

"Are you alright?" My words billowed out with the fog

of my breathe in the frosty air.

"I am so sorry. I should be the one asking you that," she replied. Her face had gone pale with the shock of the close call. She stepped forward as she spoke, "Are you okay? I mean, I am the one who caused you to have an accident."

"I'm fine. What in the world were you doing, jumping out into the middle of the road like that? Is your car broken down or something?"

The woman's car was a midnight-black, S-class Mercedes-Benz. It was a bit difficult to look at, as its color contrasted with the sun glaring off the snow so violently that the car appeared to almost vibrate.

"Well, yes and no. Oh, I don't quite know. I'm lost, which is just as bad as being broken down, but my car is fine. My GPS isn't working, and of all the stupid things, I left my cell phone back at the house. I'm very far away from home right now."

I could see the woman was not at all in her native environment. "Doesn't a car like this have some sort of internal GPS built into it?" I said, "or a replicator of some sorts? Sorry, just kidding. Um, I have a cell phone, if you want to use it."

"No, no replicator in this baby. I don't need something that produces more stuff. I've got stuff. I'm getting rid of stuff. Although having a transporter built in would be a worthy investment, actually." She laughed.

"You could fund the construction of a Stargate, too. I'd gladly be your first team member." I stood at attention, clicking my heels. At the same time, I realized how strange my comment must have seemed to this woman. "I really don't know why I am talking about sci-fi TV shows. I nearly ran over you."

The woman replied, "As crazy as it may sound, I'm pleased that it was a fellow Trekkie and Stargate fan who nearly killed me. I don't know what I was thinking. I was so worried about not knowing where I am, and about being without the use of my tech. I was overjoyed to see you coming down the road. I could talk your ear off about Star Trek and Stargate SG-1. I'm an avid fan of both shows."

"Wow, that's so great! Yup, I am a part of SG-1's long lost team, actually. I predict many hours of 'debriefing' between us, so we can compare notes on the shows."

The woman cleared her throat and straightened her shoulders. It was strange to see this smartly-dressed woman with her $150,000 car out in the middle of nowhere.

The steam from our breath was creating a menagerie of wondrous shapes. She had an engaging smile and I felt like I was in the presence of the queen of Cheshire cats. No, she was more than that. She exuded the energy of a kind-hearted leader, a person of influence. I have no idea how long we stood there at the side of the road chatting, but the absurdity of the situation reminded me of Alice In Wonderland.

This stately and poised middle-aged woman oozed authority and possessed a unique kind of beauty. Her sandy-brown hair was pulled into a tight bun and she wore a shimmering blue scarf tied artfully around her neck. She emanated a sense of focus and persuasion when she smiled, but it was her eyes that most caught and held my attention. The intensity of her gaze was mesmerizing in a way I had never experienced with any other human. Taken all together, she resembled an eighteenth-century monarch who had stepped out of another realm to make an appearance in the present time. I could not imagine what this woman did for a living or why she was so far out of her natural element.

"That's a lovely scarf you have there," I said casually. "Kashmir?"

"Shartoosh, actually, but don't tell anyone. It's quite illegal to buy or trade one of these anymore. They nearly massacred the poor antelope whose hair is used to make this precious wool. This scarf is more than 50 years old, and I can truthfully say that I did not purchase it. It was a gift from a very special grandmother in my life, once upon a time."

Another grandmother. My nose was itching, and I hoped I wasn't going to start sneezing again. "Very lovely," was all I could say. Pay attention to the riches, huh, Mary?

I still didn't know her name. "I'm just glad to know that you are not hurt. Um, my name is Elise. And you are?"

"Abigail. Abigail Rose."

"It is a joy to meet you, Ms. Rose. Listen, I don't think it's smart for us to be standing here on the side of the road like this. I know I'm a complete stranger to you, and I was almost the cause of you meeting your Maker, but if you would like to accompany me, I was on my way to eat an ice cream sundae. Want to come?"

I was shocked by my bold invitation. It's totally out of character for me to be so socially outgoing. In the last three years I had intentionally trained myself to be the complete opposite of the overly friendly person I am inclined to be.

Abigail thought for a moment, smiled, and said, "You're going to eat ice cream on a winter's day like this? You're my kinda gal. I'd be happy to accompany you. I just hope you can get your car out of that snow bank."

"It doesn't look that bad, actually. And I'm sure you have some other expensive supernatural tool in your trunk, just in case, right? I have a million questions regarding your status as a Star Trek aficionado."

"Well, it's more like an addiction. But it's a healthy addiction that keeps me happy. And I aim to be the queen of happiness. Just don't go too fast. I may have a Benz, but it isn't rigged for warp speed. Judging by the way you drive, you seem to think that you can get to another galaxy through the use of your car. Slow it down, Elise."

"Will do, Ms. Rose."

"Stop calling me that. I may be older than you, but I'm Abigail."

"Yes, ma'am. I mean, yes, Abigail."

We both laughed.

Take me to your Ice Cream leader. I am in need of reinforcement."

"Aye aye." I threw her a mock salute and we each hopped into our cars. Angela pulled out of the snow bank with ease and I got back onto the road, still unpopulated save for our two vehicles.

"It's so easy to go where the sweet richness is, eh Angela, and I am sorry you cannot partake of its form in ice cream. I'll give you an oil change instead. But the riches are really everywhere, and our Abigail back there will bring something beyond the material to the Weet Gatherings. I know it, although I doubt she knows why she's following me. I wonder what her story is? Mother, Annie, Mary, where are you and why did you send me to encounter this new Strong Weet?"

No answer. My mind was full of giant hills of vanilla ice cream, with streams of chocolate fudge rolling down.

***

My favorite old-time ice cream parlor, Joey's Gelateria, is located about five miles south of town. Joey's is a little mom-and-pop ice cream haven. The son of the original owner, also named Joey, is an older man who keeps the place just as it had been when his Italian-immigrant parents opened it in 1965. Booths with lime-green upholstered seats and varnished table tops line up on one side of the parlor, and an assortment of tables and chairs provide additional seating. The walls are adorned with an eclectic array of pictures, posters, plates, memorabilia, and souvenirs accumulated over the years. I always head for the booth where the photo of Marlon Brando in his prime is mounted on the wall at eye level. You know the one — form-fitting black t-shirt, hands pockets, casually leaning against the wall, the alluring smile, and the direct piercing gaze. Only the reality of the best hot fudge sundae can compete with the fantasies conjured by the sight of that image.

We were the only ones in the shop on that Saturday mid-morning. The Brando table was ours.

"Welcome to my dream come true," I said as we slid into the booth. "Ice cream with Marlon. Abigail, this is Marlon. Marlon, Abigail."

Abigail looked at me with raised eyebrows. "Elise you are too much." She laughed and played along, "Nice to meet you, Mr. ...?" She looked at me playfully.

"Brando."

"Right. Mr. Brando. It's a pleasure to meet you. I was watching your movies before your biggest fan here was even born."

There are no menus in Joey's, only a chalkboard above the bar listing all the scrumptious possibilities. The ice cream is homemade, back in the day, Joey senior and his wife purchased the milk for their homemade ice cream directly from several nearby farmers. These days, Joey Junior buys from a regional co-op but still makes the ice cream right there at the shop.

Abigail and I studied the menu while Joey stood behind the bar polishing a large glass sundae dish. The menu is not large, but is constantly changing, the offerings dependent on the availability and quality of ingredients, as well as Joey's culinary imagination.

Sensing that we had made our choices, Joey came over to our booth and said, "And what kind of towering mound of joy you gonna order on a day like this with your lovely friend you haven't introduced me to yet?"

Abigail and I laughed. I started to make the introduction, but she stepped in.

"I'm Abigail Rose. It is a pleasure to meet you, Joey."

"That's right, Miss Rose. It is indeed a pleasure. A fine lady like yourself is always welcome in this house."

We chatted about business, ice cream flavors, and old times for a few minutes before we placed our orders.

"Okay then," Joey said. "I'll just leave you two fine ladies to your own conversation while I conjure up your sundaes from heaven"

Abigail brought me back to the purpose of the moment.

"So, I am now going to tell you how you fit into my life, Elise."

I looked at her, impressed with her conviction.

"Go for it." The suspense of what she might reveal of understanding was wonderful.

"I don't mess around. I have always known exactly how to move, when to move, and what to move when it comes to the world of finance and business. I come from a long line of entrepreneurs, and my family practically owns this state's backbone, among other bodies. But three months ago, that all changed. I am giving away my riches. All of it."

I listened, inviting her with my silence and rapt attention to continue.

She took a deep breath and let it out slowly through slightly pursed lips before going on. "I will not leave this planet with the blood of mankind's addiction to material wealth on my soul. I have committed myself to acting in opposition to the of will my family, and what had become my own will. I have decided to transfig ... transmit ... no, I mean—"

"Transmute?" I offer.

"Yes, that's it. That's the exact word I was looking for. I intend to have all of my wealth transmuted into something more worthy and of far greater value, but I'm still figuring it out. I have wanted for many months now to make amends for all the nasty things I've supported in the past."

"Nasty things?" Joey was on his way over with two towering sundaes of perfection.

"All you need to know is that much of my family's money and my own, has helped to finance some of the biggest political figures in this country. I can't explain it, but about a year ago, I had this kind of a flash—a literal flash. I was clearly shown that all of them, and a few in particular, were just plain filth and that their goal was to degrade life on this planet to less than filth. I cannot tell you what I went through at that time to rid myself of my own nastiness, which I had made and carried within me. It was disgusting."

"Sounds like a part of healing to me." I was aware of my hand picking up the spoon to dig into the mound of icy vanilla and hot fudge, but my spirit was focused on Abigail's Glow and the way it was dancing around with my own. "It's as if you were not only shown an ocean of truth, but that you willingly chose to dive into it as well. That's extremely bold and strong of faith. How truly exciting for you!"

Abigail stared at me for a moment. "Yeah ... well ... you know ..." She shrugged her shoulders and continued. "Anyway, it felt like hell for a bit, and I won't turn your stomach by describing some of the things that my

body went through as a part of that ..." She struggled
for her word.

"Exorcism," I said. The familiarity of Abigail's experience brought warm surges of compassion through my
every cell.

"Exactly. Lord, I am so grateful you almost killed me,
Elise."

I nearly spit out my ice cream, which made us laugh
even harder than her comment did.

"It was very much an exorcism. All the things my family
has been—and is still—involved in aren't really relevant.
I'm not against wealth, or people making money and
living successfully. It's how they do it and the intention
behind it. I'm just now at the point where I want the whole
of my life to be used by God and not by greed."

Abigail closed her eyes as she took a generous bite
of her sundae. She closed her eyes and leaned into the
upholstered back of the booth as she savored the flavors
and sensations.

I remained silent, breathing in the sacred energy of
her expression.

She swallowed and returned to the conversation. "I
realize that I have been looking for whoever else might
be here on this planet and wants to live in the same way.
It's a simple way, but a good way. It feels pure."

"Yes," I responded. "I hear you speak of the core of
life, which is unmarred. It is perfection, and perfection
is simplicity. What happened then, after that period of
letting go?"

"I spent months looking for some kind of spiritual orga-
nization to support and join with, but I found nothing but
idiots and flakes who tried to coerce me into donating
thousands of dollars to their movements using the guise
of so-called spirit to push their own agendas of positive

affirmation. I even had one guy tell me that my 'inner Christ' was about to join with the photon belt, and that if I wanted to accelerate my own radiance, I could talk to someone named Adama, who apparently lives three thousand feet below the surface of the Earth."

Joey, who had come over to give us the bill, chimed in. "Actually, he got the name wrong. That would be my dead great-uncle Antonio. Even from the grave he would make anyone who believed in that nonsense light up real fast."

"Joey, I promise I'll call you and your Uncle Antonio for help the next time I get another email from these crazies. They're not just crazy though, they're dangerous." Abigail picked up the bill and began folding it absent-mindedly. What I had thought to be random angles were soon revealed to be a delicate origami flower. She stuck a twenty-dollar bill in the petals and handed it to Joey.

"No change, Joey. Thanks a bunch." Joey took the paper, did a gentlemanly sort of bow, and held the flower in his left hand, admiring it.

My spoon clinked on the bottom of my sundae dish as I scraped up the last bit of fudge. "Yes, it's dangerous to distract and divert people from the simple truth that personal power comes from God alone. There is a big industry around self-proclaimed salvation. How much more disconnected can a culture get before it all just disappears? God is too big for any one person or group of people to claim that divinity is inherent on an exclusively personal level."

Joey added, "You got to show goodness to be goodness, and you certainly can't be goodness without showing it."

"Precisely," Abigail replied. "Wow, I haven't felt this good in a long while. Joey, what do you really put into this stuff?" she asked, indicating what remained of her sundae.

"Just good old-fashioned love, that's all," Joey winked.

"Come back to Joey's Gelateria anytime, and I'll give you a big helping of it every time," he said before returning to his position behind the counter.

"Elise, I just revealed a few years' worth of my life right now, and you've barely said a word. What do you think about all of this?" Abigail dug into the last few bites of her sundae with more concentration.

"I have been swimming in it all, Abigail. There's exactness in our being together now, and I have simply been reveling in it, listening to your every word. It is with great joy that we meet again."

"Huh?"

I realized that I had almost revealed too much. "I mean that it is with great joy that I know we will meet again."

"Okay, fine, but what's your take on why we are here together now?"

"I heard you say that you are at the point where you are ready to find the others who live by the truth of heart, right?"

"Yes, and I also want each and every moment of my life to be used for whatever God wants, and for God's Will alone. I guess we're supposed to be doing some of this together."

"There will be many more Gatherings with myself and some others I know who feel pretty much the way you do. If you'd like to gather with us, those times will be just like this and even better, I promise." I got up to put on my coat.

"Phew, that's a relief." Abigail slipped into her leather coat.

"How 'bout I call you the next time we plan to gather? We'll keep it simple and use phones and computers, if you like."

Abigail scribbled down her email address and cell

phone number on a piece of paper and gave it to me as we walked out of Joey's. We were about to get into our cars when Joey stuck his head out of the front door and yelled, "And I will expect that your next Gathering might include a visit to Joey's Gelateria, eh?"

How Melody was Healed

Many months have passed, and The Great Plan continues on in its own timelessness. It is now the end of March, and we are living with the mystery of when winter in Missouri will end this particular year. In many years past, we have watched the pea plants nod in a warm spring breeze by now, but such is not the case this year. With the world-wide damage to the Creation Frequency, unpredictable weather changes seem to happen overnight. Maybe tomorrow there will be a tropical jungle here on Annica. That would be lovely, for that is the way it once was.

In the middle of our long stretch of snowy cold weather, however, there was an especially warm Gathering of the Strong Weet one Saturday here on Annica. This meeting was looked forward to with great expectation, as it was to include all of the Strong Weet currently awakened and participating actively in Weet frequency manipulation. Sit and Merta were there, of course, but Christa, Abigail, and Melody were also able to join us this time. The Gathering was as complete as possible, although it had been made clear to Din that there was still one more Weet somewhere, yet to be revealed.

The mudroom filled with wet, snowy boots and cups of tea and hot chocolate were passed around in abundance.

"Thank you for welcoming us into your home, Elise," Abigail said as she removed the wool scarf that had been muffling her mouth, neck and shoulders.

"It's so warm and cozy in here. Are those cinnamon pastries I smell?" Melody lifted her nose to inhale the enticing aroma.

"Let's just bask in the warmth of goodness here before we get started," Sit said. "What a blessing it is to see you all"

There was such a bustling energy of cheer, contentedness,

and homecoming that my little ranch-style house on Annica had never been happier. Opi, our Aussie-poodle, greeted everyone's knees with a wet nose and a wagging tail as the children bustled about taking everyone's coats. Everyone found a chair and sat down amid sighs and small talk.

Din took command as usual and brought us to order. "Alright, listen up. It has been many months since Christa, Melody, and Abigail joined with us, and it is important that we check in with each of you to learn if there is anything you wish to share, or if you have questions about your own re-discoveries. You all bring your own unique gifts to the Gathering, and we'd like to hear about them. But you're also here to listen and to do business. As happy as I am to see all of you, these Gatherings are not tea parties, okay?"

Everyone nodded in agreement.

Christa surprised us by speaking first. "I'd like to share something, if I may." Everyone became silent. Christa hardly ever spoke a word during the Gatherings.

Din nodded encouragingly and said, "Go ahead, Christa."

"Well, this isn't going to surprise any of you because it's a miracle. I waited to bring this to your attention because it was required that all of you be present. But instead of me telling you about it, I'll just show you. Excuse me." Christa set her cup of tea down, rose from her seat, and left the room.

Puzzled, the rest of just looked at each other, but we remained quiet and patient. Christa returned a few minutes later carrying a large black portfolio. It was the hardbound kind with black ribbon ties whose function is to safely store and transport works of art.

Christa laid the portfolio on the coffee table, closed her

eyes, and took a deep breath.

Before Christa could speak Melody exclaimed, "Oh, my dear Lord, it was you, Christa, wasn't it?" She smiled widely, her eyes lit with happiness.

Christa opened her eyes briefly to return the smile, then closed them for a moment's reverie. She opened them again to look once more upon the recently healed Weet.

"I did very little, Melody. It was God. And it was you who came back to us by way of the hand of the His Will."

Christa untied the folder, opened it, and held up the piece of thick white canvas for all of us to see.

It took a moment for our stunned vision to resolve the array of vibrant color into the likeness of Melody. She was arrayed in a gown made of flowers and sat delicately on a large rock. The brilliance of blue sky behind her was such that it appeared to spill beyond the confines of the painting. Every detail of each flower covering Melody's gown glowed with clarity.

"Phenomenal," Din said, his voice husky with emotion.

The rest of us remained silent, mesmerized by the energy, beauty, mastery, and magic of the painting.

Minutes passed and then, one by one, each of us moved closer to the painting to take in the details, then stepped back to sit in its radiance. Everyone except Melody.

Christa spoke again. "I started this painting three years ago. Two months ago, I met you, Melody, in person for the first time,"

Melody smiled. "I am aware, dear Christa."

Christa continued, "A wondrous thing has occurred through it. This painting is a great mystery, but I think you all can imagine what has happened."

"Uh, no, not really," Abigail said. "I'm afraid that I have no idea what you are talking about, I'm afraid I'm not as spiritually attuned as the rest of you."

"Actually, Abigail, I have no idea what Christa is referring to either," Din said, "and I'm sure that none of the rest of the group do, either. Well, with the exception of Melody, that is," Din looked at our Strong Weet who had so recently been healed from Alzheimer's.

Christa turned the painting towards herself and looked at it lovingly. "As you all know, I have an Italian grandmother, my Nonna. She's the one who first hinted to me of you, Melody, but I didn't know who it was that I was painting at first. This was even before I had begun to paint the mural of Nonna on the wall at Nene's Restaurant."

We remained silent while Christa gathered her thoughts. The painted sunshine reflected from the woman's skin, bounced off the flowers, and into the one gazing upon the painting. The woman's face was so very real, her skin weathered but alive with wisdom and beauty beyond this world.

Christa continued. "I have to explain something important before I tell you about this healing portrait, for that is what this painting is. My Nonna first began speaking to me in ways that are not natural to most people. Um, you see, she moves me now, just as she did back then, in waves. She made me realize who she was as my spirit grandmother long before I knew who she was as a woman in my ancestral family line. She has always been with me, from before the time I was a baby, and that's why I've never felt alone, never questioned why I came to Earth, or what it was that I'm called here to do."

Din cleared his throat. "Do you realize that you're probably the only one on this planet who's been given this precious gift? To maintain, with awareness, a transmission like this from the Great Tree is unheard of. Not only have you known of her throughout your childhood, you have known of your communion with her since before you came into your body."

Merta's tea cup began to rattle on the saucer she held in one hand. She brought her other hand up to silence it. "*Ai, mi'jita*, Christa. This is similar to how Pacha Mama has been with me. But I only first came to know her when she was my physical grandmother, and then stronger still after she left her body. Do you all feel what is happening in here?"

A lilting sound reminiscent of a wind chime filled the room. The chimes that usually filled the garden in spring and summer had been taken down months ago, in preparation for winter, and all the windows were closed, as it was still cold outside. Yet the sound grew in strength, emanating from a unknown source. We all heard it clearly.

Christa smiled. "Yes, of course. Nonna is here, along with quite a few others, I am sure. She wants me to get on with telling you how this painting came to be." She looked at Melody. "Melody, will you hold this as I speak?"

"With honor."

Christa rose and placed the painting on Melody's lap and the carnation-pink Glow that surrounded the older woman increased in brilliance. Once again, Annica was overwhelmed by the supernatural. Melody appeared to be sitting on the very rock depicted in the painting. Her body was transfigured into a sort of energy field. Her clothing did not appear to be made of flowers, but of bands of layered light. The colors of the bands were the same as the colors of the flowers in the painting. The living room itself became as bright as the sunny day of this captivating and healing portrait. We were witnessing the interfusion of Melody with the painting, or the painting with Melody's spirit. It was the physical process of this sacred art emerging as life. What Annie had discussed some weeks ago regarding God's doings through exclusive kinds of art became clear in that moment.

"Three years ago, I was sitting in my apartment, staring at a dew drop on the outside window pane," Christa said. "It was early morning, and there was just this one tiny little drop on the window sliding down the glass like a woman's tear. I felt Nonna, but the woman was not Nonna. Nonna never cries. I got closer to the drop, and, as I did, I could feel this woman, whoever she was, trying to come out of something but she was trapped. She was trying to speak but was unable to. The longer I watched the drop, the more I knew that it really was a tear. It was the tear of a woman asking for help from me. I set up my easel, picked up my palette, and began to bring forth this woman's spirit.

"I started to paint the tear drop, but I have to tell you, the tear drop painted itself. This was the first time in my life that I witnessed such a thing. The drop of water on the window pane transported itself through the room and pointed to the spot where I was to begin to paint a drop of silver-white-blue."

Sit was leaning forward to examine the painting. "Yes, I see it there!" she exclaimed, pointing to the upper right corner of the painting, directly above the most brilliant part of the sun.

"From there, the painting just flowed. The sunshine came out of my paintbrush, and directly led to this woman's face. I had no idea that the spirit of this woman was an actual person. I only knew that she needed to come out of something, to come back in some way. Nonna whispered to me from time to time, telling me which flowers to paint and where, but mostly I was listening to the woman. I heard her tell me what flowers were most special to her, what secrets they carried, and what it was she loved so, in this life that she knew. She kissed me the whole way through this painting. It took a long time to complete—almost a full year."

Melody spoke. "Yes, I was kissing you that whole time, Christa. You and I had such a special year. Every day, you came back to me. You were the only one who could truly hear me, and you created exactly what it was that I was telling you I needed. All of these flowers hold a specific kind of healing power. They are all keepers of timeless vibrations of the Great Tree. I needed them to be reborn somehow in this dimension, because I could not do it myself. I needed someone else of like spirit to summon them for me. I needed a physical helper to do God's work through me. That was you. After a while, you came to know what was going on, yes?"

Christa laughed, "Well, yes, after a while. In the beginning, I wasn't thinking at all, I was just streaming the communication into the palette, but I do remember the day when I suddenly saw you and I realized what it was you were emerging from. It still amazes me, Auntie Melody, how clear you were inside while you were having to live in your body with Alzheimer's."

"Yes, dear, but if you had not heard me through Nonna, I know I would still be stuck. When the Alzheimer's began to take over my body, I called out to you and to Nonna, knowing you were out here somewhere, preparing you for what was to come. I wasn't sure when you'd receive my communication. I waited through many months, the condition worsening all the while, but it wasn't too hard. I always had the gardens, and Mary and Annie, especially after I was moved to the care home. I was never truly alone. It was actually quite peaceful in a strange sort of way. The only frustrating thing, of course, is that no one could understand anything I said or did. It was a true blessing to be cared for so lovingly by Samantha Carter and those wonderful nurses. That was no accident. There are no coincidences in life."

Abigail stood up to move closer to the painting. "So, you're telling us that Christa was being used to help you heal from your Alzheimer's, and this painting is the reason you are well and with us now?" she said.

"Yes and no. God is the reason I have returned, but the Alzheimer's was part of my spiritual journey. Christa has always known her communion with God, although she never named it as such before her Nonna came through the wall."

That comment sent us reeling with laughter.

Melody looked surprised. "What? What did I say? She did come through the wall, didn't she?"

Christa replied, "Yes, she did, Auntie Melody. She did indeed. And then she went back into the wall."

"Well, let me finish," Melody said with a grin. "Christa's perfected gift of divine expression through the colors, in combination with her relationship with Nonna and her chosen commitment to listen to God as the guiding principle in her life was the fuel by which she was able to help me to come out of this. Yes, God used her, as God uses everyone for the purpose of assisting others on their journey. All sorts of opportunities to express unconditional love exist in every moment, and this is according to God's Will."

ELISE REFLECTS ON THE WISDOM OF THE STRONG WEET

Before I go to sleep each night, I take the time to review the events of the day. Lately, it has become like watching the greatest movie ever, all in a matter of five minutes or so, as the supernatural has woven itself into the mundane, or perhaps because I have acquired the ability to see the miraculous energy within the mundane.

Miracles, big and small, happen continuously for anyone who fully and completely acknowledges that God is the only One in control. This is not a power give-away as many believe, but to say that the whole of one's life belongs to God, is to be allowed access to the greatest Source of power in every aspect of personal life.

More often than not, it is the small miracles that have the greatest effect in the long run. I use these quiet moments of the evening to reflect on the tiny miracles of the day. By attending to them with conscious awareness, I can direct some of them into something truly extraordinary for all those sincere in their choice to live their life as belonging to God.

Miracles occur each and every moment of each and every day. There is no better or simpler way to aid the healing of the damage done to the Creation Frequency than to acknowledge the wondrous things that flow through the life of a believer. It is up to each one of us, to acknowledge them all, no matter their size.

On this particular evening I was thinking about Melody, Christa, and Abigail, and the particulars of our interactions with them over the past few months. I pictured their faces alight with smiles, and heard again the characteristic phrases that conveyed the nuanced grace of each of these unique spirit beings. These three new Strong Weet were growing in the understanding of their gifts and using them to work their own directed purpose within The Great Plan with grace, awareness, and humility.

We have nothing in common in terms of our worldly circumstances. We have totally different origins, cultural and ethnic roots, ages, work histories, preferences, everything. There isn't a specific spiritual upbringing that any of the Weet can identify, yet there is perfect harmony. Our Gatherings have become like a mirror in which each of us is reflected with the others as one body.

We meet not just once every month now, but once a week, to activate the next level of The Great Plan.

***

I marvel at Merta's healing in relation to the passing of her son, Marcos. She quickly affirmed her conviction that death is a lie that she would not accept, nor would she allow her emotional mind to enshroud her in it. She did not, could not, see Marcos in his true spirit form for many months, but relied on her beliefs. Merta is a woman of tremendous faith and she put her beliefs into action. She acknowledged the emotional waves crashed over her and threatened to pull her under. She stood firm and allowed the grieving to be real and as big as it needed to be, and then let it flow away like the waves on the beach, leaving her standing firm on the clean, hard sand.

We were talking about it one day, and she shared with me her prayer.

"I give this all to you, *Mi Dios*, for the good of all who are suffering, no matter what the reason. My freedom and place is in You, and I know that all people benefit from my knowing of this. I don't need to see You to know that You are my life.

"I realize there are millions of people whose lives are destroyed by their thoughts of despair, guilt, and sorrow. So many die that way. But I tell you, Elise, if that one scientist has proven to the world that our thoughts can change the very form of water molecules, then why cannot this same world see that what they carry in their minds affects all people?"

She was referring to Masuru Emoto's research as published in his book, *The Power of Water*. Merta was deeply impressed with his photographic documentation of the changes in a water sample when a paper with curses written on it was placed under the container, as compared to when a paper with blessings was placed there. This devout woman who'd had only images of Jesus The Christ and Mother Mary on her bedroom walls for years, actually had Din order her a poster bearing the image of a water molecule blessed with the phrase, Unconditional Love.

Merta has never been outspoken. She has always chosen to be as anonymous as possible, but her demeanor and her Glow speak volumes of her gift of healing.

"I can do more for people all over this world, in the beauty of my very relationship with Diosa, than I could flapping my lips about how much I think I know about Who God is. I just know what God promised, and it is real every moment of my life."

I've heard Merta speak of her knowledge of eternal life rarely, but appropriately when other people were in need of her wisdom. She truly is a beacon of life, a wondrous blessing.

***

Then there's Melody. Melody is like a spirit-presence in our lives. She doesn't just know compassion, she is compassion embodied. I and the other Strong Weet have discussed at length how each of us becomes awash in the spirit and fruit of compassion when we think of her.

Shortly after our first encounter with her at The Old Mill Care Home, Melody moved into her own house, where she sang into being yet another divine garden. She wanted a place where the land had never before been productive, deliberately seeking out land that had been considered unfit for seed to grow in, as she put it.

We all knew that she'd transform it into another mini-Eden, and she's done just that in the few short weeks she's been in her quaint little Earth home. Melody's favorite activity, besides singing forth the garden, is to visit local care facilities, hospitals, and hospices to breathe her blessed nature into the very core of the lives found there.

It's a toss-up as to who is more consistently silent at our Gatherings, Melody or Christa. The two are so in unity, and often share the exact same thought when either of them decides to express it. Din has jokingly referred to them as "our Quaker Weet," because of how beautifully quiet they are for hours on end.

***

Abigail has come to the supernatural by way of the mundane. She has set the example, demonstrating for us all the power of healing in her release from addiction to material possessions. She has not yet shown any particularly strong supernatural attunements, but in spite of that, she does not think herself as lacking or inadequate.

From an early age, Abigail knew she did not belong to her Earth family, and it was her rebellion against their worldly example that drew her into the reality of the training she was now receiving. She was quickly learning how to become what she was always meant to be and not what her earthly family had tried to warp her into.

Even though I am considerably younger than she, Abigail seemed to look to me as a mentor. She often drops in for a cup of tea and a chat between just the two of us. One afternoon not long ago, she really opened up. "As early as I can remember, I'd watch the activities of my mother and father, knowing that there was just something wrong with it all. I knew that I was there to help them, but I couldn't figure out how. I felt more at home in the kitchen with the cooks and maids than I did in the dining room where I was required to eat dinner every night. After all those years of expensive balls and gala fundraisers, all that Ivy League education, how could I ever come back to my true self, when I was living as a false temple of wealth?" she confided.

"It was painful when I learned just how my family's money was being used to support things that directly hurt enormous numbers of people. It became even more so when I realized that they knew exactly what they were doing. It took me ten years to finally break free of it. But I tell you, it's a heavenly thing to rediscover what true wealth is." She laughed and shook her head. "When I remember all of the vile, dark energy that came out of my body in the month after I decided to give away millions of dollars towards something worthy ... My God, Elise, I truly know what you mean when you say that the body carries the effects of disconnection from God.

"The process of my healing wasn't confined to just my body. I knew a long time ago that my body is merely the vehicle for my actions. My mind was the thing that carried the worst of the sickness. I tried flooding my brain with positive affirmations, but that never worked. Heck, I've never known anyone who got any benefit out of those worthless things. I couldn't pull out of years of lies by myself. Doubt about my actions kept plaguing me, even on the days when my body had respite from the physical detoxification I was going through. It was pretty intense.

On that first day, when I made the decision to write a check for a million dollars to a children's shelter, I went home with a smile on my face. But as I walked through my front door, the thought of what I had been doing for all those years really hit me. I felt my stomach begin to turn upside down and I was barely able to make it to the bathroom in time. I spent much of the next few hours in there."

Abigail and I were sitting in my parlor. We gazed out the southern window through numerous potted plants that graced the long windowsill. I touched the still-blooming winter cactus, its deep pink flowers dancing at the ends of the gently curving stems.

"Abigail, I remember you telling me that your family was alarmed when they found out that you were selling your townhouse and moving into a cottage on three acres of land. It must have been hard dealing with them."

"It's still hard. It's only been a few weeks since I sold the townhouse, Elise. Mother and Father began to attack me more with anger than with any logic. I explained to them clearly and calmly why I was rejecting my connections to their business affairs. I told them that my actions don't change my place in our family. They didn't understand. My father called my behavior 'an affront to all that he'd ever done for me.'

"It's gotten a little better over these past few days, but they still can't comprehend why I've given up my CDs, stocks, and bonds. My townhouse — which they bought for me — and millions of dollars. They think I need to seek psychiatric help, but I feel better and more at ease with myself now than I ever have."

"So how do you name the very thing that made all the

doubt disappear?"

"Aw, come on, Elise, that's easy." She took a long sip of her warm cinnamon tea.

"Well?" I smiled.

"The thing that makes life simple, sweet, and totally perfect is transforming this body of mine into a thing for God to use for whatever it is that God wants. That is enough for me."

A Love Letter from Mary

Let it be crystal clear that each and every healing, no matter how small, directly affects the whole of life on this planet and throughout all universes. If you find this hard to believe or to understand, re-read the section on the Great Tree. Study a photograph of the Milky Way Galaxy and see just how tiny the Earth is in relation to the rest of the galaxy. There are trillions of galaxies in this universe alone, and even more enormous suns, far greater in size than our own, each casting its light on this tiny speck of a planet. Read a few articles about biology and learn how the nuances and intricacies of the life of Earth are interwoven into the web of growth, decay, and rebirth throughout the cosmos. Saturate your mind with the knowledge that the light that gives life to your body and mind is a tiny, yet vital part of the endless expanse of light around you. Read and study with eyes of life that are capable of seeing the complete, enormous creation of which you are an intrinsic part.

Your life belongs to life. Spend more hours of each day in nature to let the wisdom of that statement sink into your consciousness. Believe that you are in communion with all life now.

There is little time left for humanity to continue its stroll down the self-centered path its people and societies have created and maintained for centuries. The weight of the balance is near to tipping. It is too dangerous now for even one more day of superficial emotional thinking, past-living addiction, and adolescent meanderings of doubt regarding God's Presence to continue. Earth's remaining few years are flashing by, and before humanity knows it, the final message will be spoken:

The countdown has ended. Time on Earth is no longer. Now receive the consequences of your thoughts and activities — either the wonder-filled and glorious, or the unspeakable devastation.

It is time to live for the eternal reality of God's being in the timelessness of the here and now. It is time for everyone on this world to devote their life to God.

Be conscious of every single tiny and wonderful thing that occurs at every level — within your body and mind, personal life, relationships, the world. Most of all, be attuned to the majesty and wonders of nature around you. The key is to know that all goodness finds its source in Creator.

This acknowledgment will feed your spirit within your new awareness of life. By giving all the praise and glory to God healings will become more profound and miraculous for you and everyone.

Mankind has been living for millions of years in the collectively-induced belief that suffering is what rules life on this planet, but God has always tenderly observed each and every person on Earth, caring for all with supernatural love, and expecting that more would return to everlasting Life.

Let this not be the last civilization. Commit to making your every moment one in which the healings abound. Commit to life. Commit to God.

WORDS OF ENCOURAGEMENT

Mary has requested that this section be included as reassurance to everyone that there is Hope in this world, and to leave an important lesson as this volume of *The Diary* draws to a conclusion. Take this knowledge and hold it in your heart, ponder its meaning, and be on the watch for those special beings it speaks of. They are indeed present on Earth, and their mission is to guard the continuance of the human species.

***

I am Din, a member of the Family Triad whose primary duty is to relay a message of hope and warning from God to the peoples of this planet. I have not always been as I am today. Before my Awakening, and the subsequent alterations to the physical body in which I reside, I was like any other person walking this world. Physically and emotionally I was always just a little bit different, but I also had much in common with other human beings. Spiritually, however, I was always very different.

Since my spiritual journey began many years ago, I have been given many trials and ordeals. Along the way, my friends and my family commented often that they had never seen one person experience the things that I had in one single human life. Whether or not I learned what I was supposed to learn through those events is a matter for debate; the fact that I got through them is a certainty. Of course, I realize today that I had help from Mary, Annie, a few other Heavenly Beings, and, of course, God.

That being said, there are hundreds, if not thousands of books on the market today, attesting to the fact that a large portion of Earth's population, while not going through as many trials as I, have experienced similar ones, and worse. The one factor in common is that they all made it through, passed whatever tests were thrown at them, and became in some respects better for having done so.

Many lessons can be learned from passing the tests that "life, the universe and everything" puts to us, but my purpose is not to discuss what those tests might be, or what we may learn from the outcomes, but to ask instead, "How in the world were we able to get through it all?"

I've asked that question on many occasions and I must confess that during my earlier years I had little success finding an answer. The best I could say was, "I guess God just got me through it all." But then I was always forced to ask, "How? How the heck did God do it? How did He get me through it?" Which is kind of like asking, "How does God work?" Which is, of course, way beyond the capacity of any conscious human mind to figure out. I didn't have Mary or Annie actively in my life back in those days. I didn't even really have the real Me in my life back then. I was simply DH, and I had to go about life daily filled with countless questions and concerns, just like any other person.

So, I ended up doing what a lot of people do when they have something that is bothering them to the point of distraction. I went ahead with the God confrontation bit and asked Him directly just how in the world He had gotten me through all of the stuff I had been through. I specifically remember telling Him, "You know, God, I really shouldn't even be alive! I've done some pretty dumb things, and I've been in some pretty unfriendly situations." Then I sat back and fully expected God to answer me. And why not? That's what I had learned in Sunday School as a child, and if it was true that God answered kids when they prayed, why wouldn't He do the same now that I was an adult?

God did answer me. In fact, He started streaming a ton of thoughts and answers into my head that seemed to deal directly with what I was asking. I remember pressuring God with more questions even as I received the first of those thoughts. I just couldn't keep quiet.

"How do You communicate with me just as I am about to accidentally step off a cliff?"

"How do You tell me I should or shouldn't do this or that because my own decisions might get me into deep trouble?"

"Was that You Who saved my butt when that truck almost plowed into my car at that four-way stop last year?"

Of course, one of the main ways God communicates with us is through other people. Friends and relatives, bosses, co-workers, teachers, everyone we come into contact with is a possible channel for God to use to get His message to us. Even if they are 100% evil people, God can use them as examples of what not to do and how not to be.

I remember times when a friend said something to me at just the right time that made me think twice about doing something really stupid. I remember talking to priests and pastors and to those who had supposedly attained a higher degree of spiritual understanding than I had at the time, and they were able to dissuade me from making decisions or taking action that would have had long-term negative consequences that would affect me for the rest of my life.

Even though it's wonderful when friends come through for us with great counsel in times of need, we should not depend solely upon human beings for our Spiritual welfare and/or rescue. There are "others" we should be aware of who serve us in that capacity.

I am referring to the countless number of what this world refers to as angelic beings, who work tirelessly behind the scenes in an effort to guide and protect people throughout their daily lives. The term, angelic being, brings to mind several images depending on one's personal faith, philosophy, or general outlook on the universe. While it is possible for these great beings to appear in any form they wish, angels do not run around the world willy-nilly, popping in on people at the drop of a hat or, as some would have you believe, anytime and every time a human snaps their finger. Angels are extremely powerful beings who are given very specific tasks, and who are answerable only to the commands of God.

Angels have been around since the beginning of time. In fact, they were a part of the original Creation. They have served The One God without question, for billions of years, not only in this universe, but all other universes as well.

There are two principle forms of other-dimensional beings that fall into the category of what humans call angels: Holy Angels and Guardian Angels. I've heard some refer to their loved ones who have passed away as angels. That is simply not the case. The spirits of friends and family who have gone before us are not in the same category as angelic beings, and although they can be active in watching over us from the other side, they cannot do what angels can do.

There are five primary functions of Angelic Beings:

1. To DELIVER VERY IMPORTANT MESSAGES from God. Please note the emphasis. Angels were not created to help you find a boyfriend, or to bail you out of silly problems you get yourself into.

2. To PROTECT GOD'S GREAT PLAN throughout the ages.

3. To PROTECT HUMAN BEINGS in times of serious

distress.

4. To PETITION God for the healing of a human body, or even the healing of a nation. Notice the emphasis on the word, petition. Only God heals. Period. Even these powerful Spirit Entities called Angels are incapable of healing anyone or anything. That is not their function.

5. To DESTROY anything that is contrary to The Great Plan as it moves along in time.

The Holy Angels, also known as Archangels, are the highest form of angel. They are quite powerful, but they can only work within the perfect Will of God. There are only two of these mentioned in the Christian Bible, Michael and Gabriel. The first of these is Michael, whose primary function is divine protection. Although Michael is not the being's real name, the biblical descriptions of this powerful angel are accurate and he will, in fact, be quite active during the End Times if The Great Plan comes to a bitter end for this world, instead of the hoped-for end described in these *Volumes* of *Mary's Diary*. Michael is the *Malak Tsedek*, the Messenger of Justice.

The created being humans refer to as Gabriel is the other Holy Angel. Gabriel, also not the real name, has been given the task of delivering serious messages from God to Earth. Gabriel is the principal Healing Angel as well as a messenger.

Some teach that there are several more archangels, but that is not the case. That is not to say, however, that Michael and Gabriel are the only two angels. There are indeed many angels, without titles or names, who act as guardian angels on this planet every moment of every day.

The guardian angel is a phenomenon found within the recognized sacred scriptures of nearly every religion on earth. Guardian Angels do exist but, again, they do not go into action every time a human snaps a finger. They, too, respond only to the command of God, and for very specific purpose. The Guardian Angel is a companion for life. This wonderful being is the personification of love and loyalty in regard to care and protection in the physical state, but pure love does not always bail a person out of trouble. Sometimes it allows the person to learn from their mistakes.

Guardian Angels are the most active of all angels. Some humans are quite aware of this angel in their lives, having had an experience that could only be explained by the intervention of such a being. The scope of the assignment of protection a Guardian Angel is given is comprehensive—a full-time job, to say the least. Most of the instances in a human's life that require the intervention of a Guardian Angel go completely unnoticed

In *The Lost Revelation*, the second volume of *Mary's Diary*, I revealed the concept of what I call earth guides. I want to share a quote from that page in order to emphasize a concept that Mary, Annie, and I pray will stay with you as you go forward from this moment in your lives.

> An Earth Guide is one who, although
> housed within a physical form, is con-
> cerned more with the supernatural plane/
> dimension and with the welfare of the
> spirit nature rather than the physical.

What exactly is it that angels are primarily concerned with? While angels are not housed in a physical form, they, too, are concerned more with the spiritual plane/dimension and with the welfare of the spirit rather than the physical. Since the job description for the Weet is exactly the same as for the angels and earth guides, what does that make them? Weet are highly advanced earth guides and physical angels whose primary duty is to see that their job description is fulfilled.

Remember that there are three types of Weet on this world. The ten Strong Weet and the fourteen Secondary Weet are very powerful in their nature because of their direct lineage back to the Founders of this world and also because of their friendship with the Family Triad. The third type, the Support Weet, also carry some direct lineage to the Founders. While individually of lesser power than the Strong and Secondary Weet, they are important in their own right. There are literally thousands, perhaps millions, of these Weet taking up their positions every day, all around this globe, and their power lies in their combined dedication to God's Will and to The Great Plan.

The fact that you are presently reading *Volume Three* of this series means that it is highly probably that you are, at the very least, one of the Support Weet. You would not have been moved to read beyond *Volume One* if you didn't believe it at some level. These books are not your common science fiction, nor are they fantasy. They are very real. They are Truth. The prophecies and predictions found in the pages of these volumes are coming true exactly as they were revealed. Every day, new events happening in the world are proving beyond the shadow of a doubt that The Diary of Mary Bliss Parsons is, perhaps, one of the most important works ever to have been written. In it is found the True destiny of mankind and, more importantly, how mankind can help to bring about a happy ending to it all and save the world in the process.

A MATTER OF PERSPECTIVE

During a break midway through a presentation at a local college, I happened to be standing next to a window overlooking the lawns outside. The building was an old gymnasium built somewhere around the turn of the last century or before and later converted for use as a lecture hall. It retained all the charm that many old buildings might have — beautiful wood floors, high ceilings, and especially the windows. I looked through the wavy old glass and wondered how many windows had been broken in the early days when students still played basketball inside.

As I leaned against the window sill and gazed out at the beautiful lawn, I began to look not so much at the sky and the trees and the buildings, but at the lawn itself which is at eye level because the floor of the gym is about four feet below the surface of the ground. My attention became riveted on a frequently overlooked — pardon my pun — little world. Because of my ability to "see" in ways different from others, I was able to take in ad fully appreciate the magical sight that lay before me. I was spellbound. The more I peered at this little microcosm of life, the less aware I was of anything else going on around me. I began to notice, perhaps for the first time in my life, the miraculous wonders that such a mundane little patch of earth could reveal to the human eye.

The first thing to grab my attention was a tiny black ant wandering around in an apparently carefree and meaningless fashion. He didn't appear to have a destination at all, he just rambled from left to right and north to south and west to north, easily climbing over any obstacle he encountered — obstacles that, if scaled to human size, would be nearly insurmountable to us.

Now, I know the ant surely had some sort of purpose

in mind as he wandered around like that. Perhaps he was looking for a new source of food to take back to his colony, or a water source. But it wasn't so much his purpose or intent that mesmerized me as it was the obstacles he had to overcome. Two thoughts occurred to me. First of all, from the ant's viewpoint these obstacles varied in size from merely large to gargantuan. Every little rock he climbed was, proportionately, the size of a large boulder. The larger rocks were mountainous.

Another consideration is that the actual ground of any lawn is strewn with various objects rarely noticed by human eyes. When people encounter large physical obstacles, they usually go around them, or go back the way they came, but nothing stops an ant's forward progress. Everything an ant meets along the path of its life is not only something very large, it is something the ant has to climb over. Something he must conquer. Even simple blades of grass must seem like a forest to an ant.

As I watched the little fellow travel through the grass, I realized that a slight breeze kept the blades in constant motion. The ant was forced to bob and weave with every step just to make his way through them. I wondered what that must seem like to that poor little guy? Thousands of large green protuberances vibrating and waving all around him in every direction, a veritable sea of translucent, sun-glowing, massive green knife blades, some as tall as the Empire State Building, swaying every which way around and beside and above him in wild abandon. Like a psychedelic light show from the sixties only with an added touch of mortal danger.

The little ant didn't seem at all disturbed. At one point I even saw the little creature climb up on one of the swaying blades of grass and ride it for a while. I wonder if he enjoyed the experience?

So, what does all this have to do with this book? Plenty. The volumes of *Mary's Diary* are filled with content concerning the principles of metaphysics. The word *metaphysics* is not a bad word. It is defined most simply as something that is beyond the physical. Although an ant is a physical creature, the inner mechanics governing how an ant processes its physical life must certainly be of a non-physical nature.

It is assumed by most scientists that ants don't think like human beings think. It is believed that they don't feel emotion like people feel emotion. In fact, the consensus is that ants process just about everything differently than humans. Scientists believe that ant behavior is purely instinctive, guided by the chemistry contained in their tiny brains—"If they even have brains," as one scientist said.

Yet, since my experience with the ant outside the gymnasium window, I find ants appealing. It's not the way they act and react physically that I'm intrigued by, it's their apparent outlook on life. I mean, if an ant is just in it for the instinctual inner command to "bring home the bacon," so to speak, then why did that one get up on that blade of grass and act as if it were on a ride at Disneyland? Perhaps there is more to this ant stuff than meets the eye. Maybe there's something people can learn about themselves, if they take the time to go beyond the physical—and the scientific—theories about ants and dabble for a while in the metaphysical, which, remember, is where a whole lot of this book resides.

Is it all just instinct? Consider the following traits of ants. Is it possible that there is something behind what scientists observe as the typical characteristics of the common ant that proves it to be more than simply an instinctual creature? Could it be that ants might even be superior to humans in some ways

Unlike a lot of people, ants are mega-producers. They're always busy, they're never lazy, and they don't make excuses. Many human beings spend half their time on the job doing work of poor quality and the other half making excuses for it. I've never seen an ant take a cigarette break, go out on strike, or perform its task poorly. That's called responsibility and it produces quality results.

The efforts of ants, being the tiny creatures they are, generate very little actual force, but their relative strength is such that they can accomplish feats far beyond the ability of any human.

A few weeks ago, I brought home over a hundred concrete pavers, so that Annie and I could build a patio at the entrance to the Annica Garden. I'm not sure how much each block weighed, but I could only carry one or two at a time, and when I got through with the job, every muscle in my body ached. By contrast, an ant could easily have done the job in only two or three trips. Incidentally, Annie spent the time floating around "supervising," and never lifted one block, even though she could have moved them all at once with great ease.

An ant has little strength compared to a man. Issues of mechanics and scale aside, one thing that makes a difference is that the ant, unlike the man, concentrates its strength on one particular thing at any given time, so that its strength is maximized. An ant uses all its strength on one thing in order to get the job done. It doesn't multitask. It doesn't waste time and energy like we do. Perhaps some of it is instinctive, as in the case of storing up food for the winter, but I wonder... is it instinct or is it an inner guidance mechanism that is more like intelligence — or the directive Spirit of God?

Are the ants really thinking ahead? If so, this is a good lesson for humanity. Emergency, recession, inflation, depression, ill health, old age, and retirement—I'm not talking about storing up treasures on earth, I'm talking about careful maintenance of what God has loaned to mankind. Just as the natural resources of Earth are being abused and used up at an incredible rate, there is no guarantee that when the time comes to face common emergencies, the means to do so will be there. Every human being on Earth should be concerned about not just the future of the planet, but about their personal future, as well. This is a lesson that has not yet taken hold even after thousands of years of human trial and error. Something else, usually of a selfish or personally profitable nature, has always come along and put itself in the way of common sense and self-preservation. If this world is truly facing the imminent destruction Mary has warned of, then the prudent thing to begin immediately would be a personal analysis of one's self, and to take action to change that which needs to be changed. People must first correct themselves individually—or at least begin the effort—before they can work together with sufficient purity and strength to aid in the correction of the Creation Frequency. As Mary has said, there is a specified portion of the population of the planet that must participate in this purification process in order to show God that they are serious about saving their own home world. Humanity must place the recognition and worship of God at the top of their priority list, along with the cleanup after and the elimination of their destructive activities. If the people of Earth find other mundane activities and diversions to be more important than God, then so be it. Free will is always honored. Keep in mind, though, that the consequences of free will are always honored as well.

Ants also teach us the subtle arts of participation and cooperation. When they work, they work together as a unit in total harmony one with the other. No bickering about one ant having to carry more of the load than the next ant. No concern about Bob Ant making more money than Natalie Ant. No petty jealousies over work hours and tasks. They've just got that peanut butter sandwich lying there, and they know what has to be done.

In Uganda, villagers tie food from ropes at the end of tree limbs high in treetops so the animals can't get to it. But the ants climb the tree, crawl down the rope to the food, and then they grab on to one another and make an ant ladder all the way from the food package at the end of the tree limb to the ground beneath. Then more ants can easily crawl up along the bodies of their fellow ants and get to the food. Up and down they go until the food has been successfully removed from the tree and transported to the ant's storage mound. This entire process takes place in just a few hours, so that when the villagers come out to get their food the next morning, nothing is left but the rope.

Think of what the human race could accomplish if it copied the ant—if people could learn to lay aside their petty differences and jealousies and cooperate with each other as one body. That is what God wants, and it is a major key to the preservation of the human race.

Not once in the pages of the three volumes of Mary's Diary, has there been any mention of "racial identity." In the Eyes of God there is only one race, and that is the human race. Earth is the only planet in the entire galaxy that is concerned with the division of races. Race is not a thing of the past on other planets—it was never there to begin with. Isn't it time humanity finally grew up? Racial problems are one of the principle causes of distortions to the Creation Frequency.

When flood, wind, or predator destroys an ant colony,

the ants rebuild it immediately. They don't stop to vote about it. They don't seek the opinion of a neighboring colony. They just get the job done.

I once tried an experiment where I deliberately destroyed an ant colony. I didn't hurt the ants, I just gently leveled the ant mound and filled in the hole. It was quite large, and the damage I did was severe enough that it would have taken years to repair had the same thing happened to a human city . Within two minutes I saw the tiny head of a worker ant pop up through the dirt and sand that had covered his nest. A few seconds later, dozens of ants were streaming out the hole as if nothing had happened.

So, what did I do? I leveled it again. And again. And again. Seven times I destroyed the colony mound, and each time, I attempted to make it harder for the ants to dig their way out, including placing obstacles like small pieces of concrete and bricks in the way. Nothing stopped them. Here would come little Andy Ant, followed by all his buddies, and within minutes the nest was back in order. I watched as a small group of the ants sectioned themselves off from the others, grabbed onto the concrete and brick objects, and carried them away as if they were pieces of paper. And not only did they remove the objects from blocking the entrance, they used them to fortify the perimeter around the new nest!

The ants didn't just move out of the neighborhood. They continued to rebuild the same nest over and over again. I suppose if I had destroyed it a thousand times, they would still be there today. That's perseverance. They had chosen that particular location to support their colony and it apparently had great significance, so they weren't about to allow a mere two-legged giant the pleasure of taking that away from them. They persevered in their efforts to rebuild and retain their home until the human got tired, felt silly, gave up, and went back to his own nest.

Perseverance is one of those things that insures the preservation of the species, be it ant or human. I realize that much of this discussion deals with the physical, but just how far is the leap to bring the metaphysical or even the spiritual into the picture? Not very.

Every credible religion on earth professes all of the qualities I have mentioned or implied as being qualities that are inherent in spiritual endeavors as well: personal strength, management or stewardship skills, perseverance, creativity, participation, and cooperation.

Those things that are "beyond the physical" cannot be separated from the spiritual. Everything a human being attempts in life, everything they think or do or desire to create must all be considered from a matter of perspective. So much of what is done as a human species is so grand and glorious in humanity's eyes, and yet the little ant has been outdoing humans, in many respects, for millions of years. Even though all that mankind does, just as all the ants do, may appear superficially to be physically motivated, these activities really find their genesis in the spiritual realm. Could it be that the "Secret of Life" lies not in the pursuit of entertainment or the human ego, but in the study of Nature?

Some Closing Thoughts

A few things mentioned in *Volume One, The Strong Witch Society*, were mentioned once and never discussed again, like completely eliminating the need for fossil fuels by creating enough power to energize this world forever from a handful of common desert jasper, and the like. Some things were left unexplained because certain gifts can only be given when humanity has proven to be worthy of owning them. If certain knowledge was shared now, mankind would no doubt find a way to either capitalize on it, or to use it for nefarious purposes, or both. The Creation Frequency has been damaged enough as it is and we will not add to that damage by giving humans still one more thing to abuse.

Take a step back and look at the bigger picture. Rather than seeking to acquire specific and powerful secret knowledge, is it not better to make the message of these books a priority in your life? If you answer in the affirmative, and you begin to alter your lifestyle, returning to the worship of God and teaching others to do the same, then you will receive the withheld information in due time. You will also enjoy all of the benefits promised in *Mary's Diary* for having been a faithful student of the cosmic knowledge found therein. If you do not answer correctly—or worse, do not even care—then we can no longer sustain you in any way, and we will be asked to release you to the alternative.

Several Strong Weet were mentioned in the course of the three volumes of *The Diary of Mary Bliss Parsons*. They are, Annie, Mary, Din, Sit, Merta, Melody, Christa, Abigail, and of course, Elise, who co-authored *Volume Two: The Lost Revelation* and this volume as well. But you will also notice that we have listed here only nine of the ten that exist in this world. There is still one Strong Weet "out there" somewhere who has not been introduced. Where is she? Who is she?

Of the fourteen Secondary Weet, only seven have been Awakened as of this writing, leaving seven more to be accounted for. Who are they? They and the tenth Strong Weet are all to be found among the individuals who have read all three volumes, including this one, but have not as yet Awakened. We, The Family Triad, already know who they are and where they live. We have known their identities since before we began to write these books and we have remained silent, as it is necessary for them to Awaken on their own without our help. We can only encourage all of those who have read these books, and all who will read them within the next few months. Listen to your heart. Listen to the WHO that you really are. Hear what you are telling your own soul about what has been revealed to you in *The Diary*.

Although *Mary's Diary* was originally intended to end with volume three, there remains much information to be shared with those who wish to learn and benefit from it. Since there are thousands of Support Weet still in the process of Awakening, we also believe that it might be beneficial to create a fourth volume in order to facilitate those Awakenings. With the help of Mother H and Annie, we are working on that volume even now.

If you feel that you are Awakening, you may contact us through any one of our Facebook pages: The Strong Witch Society, DH Parsons, DH Parsons; Bliss-Parsons Institute. You can also reach us at the Bliss-Parsons Institute website: www.bliss-parsons.com. This website will be growing and evolving with the progression of the final years of The Great Plan. Many of the details of The Great Plan that were intentionally left out of *Mary's Diary* will be explained on the website as they come to light in the near future.

And they will come to pass.

For those who have truly Awakened, your contact will begin for you a journey that few on this planet will ever take. It will be a personal journey from the point where you now reside in Earth-time, to your ultimate destiny in the timeless expanse of your own wonder-filled future.

The enormity of knowledge and wisdom that is still within the reach of humanity beckons you now to receive the healing of God, opening the scrolls of revelation yet to come.

The degree to which people choose to love God is the only deciding factor for the future of Earth.

The fate of this planet now rests solely on the shoulders of humanity itself.

***

ABOUT THE AUTHORS

DH Parsons

DH Parsons—educator, inspirational speaker, and spiritual counselor—holds several university and institute degrees and awards, including a master's degree in education and doctoral degrees in comparative religions and transcendental theory. He has taught art, journalism, English, and history in both private and public schools, held positions as dean of students and administrator in public middle and high schools.

Dr. Parsons currently divides his time between his writing, spiritual counseling, and engagements as an inspirational speaker throughout the mid-western United States.

Elise R. Brion

While Elise R. Brion has earned several university and institute awards and degrees, including a doctorate in religion, she has found her true vocation as a singer-songwriter and inspirational speaker.

Elise is no stranger to miracles of physical and spiritual healing in her own life and in the lives of others. She shares her gifts through recordings of her original songs, and in healing seminars presented throughout the state where she lives.

Website: www.eliserbrion.com

Facebook: Elise R. Brion Ministries-Infinite Healing NOW

Made in the USA
Middletown, DE
19 October 2020

22358904R00139